Across the Rio Grande

Raymond D. Mason

Across the Rio Grande

Copyright © 2009 by Raymond D. Mason

All rights reserved. No part of this book may be used or reproduced by any means, graphic, electronic, or mechanical; including photocopying, recording, taping or by any information storage retrieval system without the written permission of the publisher/author except in the case of brief quotations embodied in critical articles and reviews.

Raymond D. Mason books may be ordered through authorized booksellers associated with Mason Books or by contacting:
Books sold through authorized book stores,
or personalized, autographed copies by:

E-mail: RMason3092@aol.com

Or by phoning your order to:

(541) 679-0396

This is a work of fiction. All characters, names, incidents, organizations, and dialogue in this novel are either the products of the author's imagination or are used fictitiously.

Cover by Raymond D. Mason

Printed in the United States of America

Books by This Author

The Long Ride Back
Return to Cutter's Creek
Ride the Hellfire Trail
Brimstone; End of the Trail
Brotherhood of the Cobra
A Walk on the Wilder Side
Night of the Blood Red Moon
The Woman in the Field
Day of the Rawhiders
Last of the Long Riders
The Mystery of Myrtle Creek
In the Chill of the Night
Yellow Sky, Black Hawk
Beyond Missing
Aces and Eights
8 Seconds to Glory
Four Corners Woman
Corrigan
A Motive for Murder
Send in the Clones
Murder on the Oregon Express
Night Riders
Too Late To Live
The Secret of Spirit Mountain
Rage at Del Rio
Beyond the Picket Wire
The Tootsie Pop Kid
Streets of Durango (The Lynching)

Raymond D. Mason

1

Crystal City, Texas – 1875

The big sorrel gelding kicked up a trail of dust that hung suspended in the hot, Texas air due to the absence of any breeze whatsoever. The man aboard the lathered animal used his reins to urge the horse on. Looking back over his shoulder occasionally the rider checked the trail behind him for any sign of the posse that had been pursuing him since he'd held up the freight office in Crystal City.

Suddenly the horse slowed up on its own as it began to limp badly. Knowing that the animal could not go on, the rider began to look for a place to make a stand against the pursuing posse. He spotted his battlement just off the road a couple of hundred yards. It was a rock formation that would offer him all the protection he would need to make a stand...until his food and water ran out; not to mention his ammunition.

He reined the horse off the narrow stagecoach road and towards the rock formation. Halfway there, however, he dismounted and grabbed his rifle, saddlebags, and canteen and ran the rest of the way on foot. The horse stopped and began to feed on what little dry grasses it could find.

The man reached the cleft in the rocks just as the posse topped the hill some four hundred yards away.

They didn't notice the rider-less horse until they were almost even with where it had left the road. The sheriff looked in the direction of the sorrel and called back to the other members of the posse.

"Over there," the sheriff yelled. "He's taken to the rocks."

The posse quickly swung off the road and headed towards the rock formation where the bandit was holed up. When they were approximately a hundred yards away the first shot rang out. One of the posse members yelled out in pain, "I'm hit." That's all it took for the others to dismount and run for cover.

"You hurt bad, Tom," the sheriff called out?

"No, I don't think so. It's my shoulder, but it just creased me," the man replied.

"Bill, take care of Tom, will you? The rest of you men keep your head down. He can't have much water and with this heat, that hombre is going to be getting awful thirsty before too long."

"Sheriff, we're going to get mighty thirsty as well. I didn't bring any water with me. What bout you other men? Did any of you remember to bring water along," the man asked?

Out of the ten man posse only three men had brought canteens of water with them.

"Sheriff, we'll have to send someone for some water. What do you want us to do?"

"Let's wait a little and see what he intends to do. Maybe he'll see that he's cornered with no where to run and give up peaceably."

"I don't think so; not after shooting old man Willoughby. If the old guy dies he's facing a murder charge," the man replied.

"He may not know that, though. He shot Willie as he was riding out of town and firing wildly, remember that. I'll see if I can talk some sense into him," the sheriff argued.

The sheriff cupped his hands around his mouth to form a sort of megaphone effect.

"Hey, Mister...why don't you save yourself a lot of pain and suffering and just give up. All you're wanted for right now is armed robbery. If you force our hand some of us could get hurt, or killed. Then you'd be facing a rope," the sheriff called out.

"I ain't about to spend the next ten to fifteen years sitting in some prison cell. No, I'll stay right here. If you try and rush me a lot of you are going to die...so think about that before trying something stupid," the outlaw called back.

"He ain't coming out, Sheriff. Why don't I go back to town and bring out a buckboard full of food and water. Wait till his tongue starts to swell in his mouth and he'll want to give up," one of the deputies said.

"You're right Jim. Go ahead and make the run. He ain't gong no where and neither are we," the sheriff answered.

"I'll be back in an hour or so. Is there anything else you want me to bring back?"

"Yeah, go by the hardware store and see if Clyde's got some dynamite. If he does, bring a couple of sticks with you; but don't forget the blasting caps. We'll dynamite him out of those rocks," the sheriff said wryly.

"How are we going to get close enough to heave the dynamite sticks into the rocks?"

"Nightfall will take care of that," the sheriff grinned.

7

"I'd better get a move on," the deputy said and moved towards his horse.

The sheriff called after him, "Bring the buckboard that's behind the jail. Before this thing is over we might need it to haul some wounded back to town."

"I will."

The sheriff watched his deputy mount up and head back in the direction of Crystal City. It would be at least an hour before he could get into town and back with the supplies, so if he could talk the outlaw into giving himself up it would sure make it a lot better.

"Hey, pardner, you wouldn't mind telling me your name, would you," the sheriff called out.

"Yeah, I do. Why should I make your job easier for you? If you knew my name you'd be able to post it on wanted posters and send it all over Texas...so when I escape from this standoff I'd have those posters to contend with."

"Well, it was just a thought. I wanted to know what to put on your tombstone, that's all."

The sheriff took a better look at the rock formation that housed the bandit. He suddenly realized that should there be a narrow passageway through the rocks; the man they had cornered might very well be able to sneak out when night fell.

Looking around at the men who formed the hastily put together posse, he spotted a man in which he had confidence; his other deputy, Brent Sackett.

"Brent," the sheriff called out in a loud whisper; just loud enough to get Brent's attention.

"Yeah, what is it, Ben?"

"I want you to circle around and make sure that hombre doesn't sneak out the back door of that formation. I'd hate to lose him after having him cornered like this," the sheriff explained.

"Okay, I'll do just that. One thing though...if I get a good, open shot at him do you want me to take him out?"

"Yeah, but whatever you do...don't miss."

Brent painstakingly worked his way around to the back of the rock formation. From his vantage point he could see that there was, indeed, a passageway through the rocks. As the deputy took up a position that would give him the best view of the 'back door' he began to formulate a plan.

The freight office had a good amount of cash in the safe when it was robbed. Since this was the only man involved in the robbery, there was a good chance that he still had the money with him. He really hadn't had a chance to bury the money anywhere; that was for sure. This might be a perfect set up for an enterprising individual such as himself.

The more the young deputy thought about it, the more appealing the idea became. He had taken his share of the spoils of war while fighting for the South; this was a lot like that. Besides, who was to know if the bandit was dead?

Finally he made up his mind as to what he would do. He moved down the rocky slope making sure that the man who was holed up couldn't see him. Slowly he made his way to the back of the rocky fortress. Once there he looked around on the ground for a good sized rock that he could use as a distraction.

Finding a loose rock about the size of the palm of his hand, he threw the rock atop the formation. It made a loud hard thump when it hit and then rolled around making it sound like someone had scaled the rock face. The ploy worked better than he'd expected.

The bandit came hurriedly out of his hiding place with his pistol drawn and looking upwards in the direction from which the noise had come. By the time he realized that he was fully exposed to anyone who might be at the back of the rocky fortress it was too late.

Sackett didn't say a word as he squeezed the trigger of his Winchester rifle. The bullet knocked the bandit backwards a good six feet. When the man hit the ground he was stone cold dead. Sackett wasted no time in hurrying to the dead man and grabbing his pistol.

He fired the pistol into the air twice and then dropped the gun by the dead man's body. He moved quickly between the rocks to where the bandit had first taken his position. There lying on the ground was the saddlebags next to the canteen. The man's rifle was leaning against the rock wall.

Sackett grabbed the saddlebags and opened up the flaps. There were four bundles of wrapped one hundred dollar bills in one side of the bag and at least two fists full of loose bills of different denominations in the other compartment.

Quickly Sackett removed all the wrapped bundles, but left about half of the loose bills in the saddlebags. He hurried back through the narrow passageway and once he was back where the dead man lay, stuffed a few of the loose bills into the man's pockets.

Looking around the area he saw the perfect hiding place for the bundles of bills; a hollowed out stump. Placing the money inside the stump, he covered it with some loose brush that was nearby. Grabbing a loose branch he wiped away his boot prints from the loose soil and then tossed the branch atop the others that covered the stump.

One more added touch and he could call the posse up. He grabbed the bandit's gun and fired two more shots at the rock where he had first taken up his position. The ricocheting bullets made zinging sounds as they glanced off the hard surface of the rock. One more shot from his long gun and then he let out a triumphant yell.

"I got him," Sackett yelled.

He moved to the front end of the rocky formation and out into the open, holding his rifle in the air.

"I got him, Ben. He's dead," Sackett called out.

"Come on men," the sheriff said and the posse members all hurried to where Deputy Sackett was waiting.

"Where is he, Brent," the sheriff asked when he reached his deputy?

"He's back there; he's dead."

The sheriff and the others hurried back to where the dead man lay and formed a half circle around the dead body. Looking around the area, the sheriff asked, "Where's the money?"

The men all began to look around the area while the sheriff knelt down and started going through the dead man's pockets.

"Here's some of it," the sheriff said as he pulled the crumpled up bills from the dead man's pockets.

"There's got to be more than this, though," the sheriff said as he held the bills in his hand. He then added, "Say, Brent, did you see the man's war bags?"

Sackett walked back to where the sheriff and the others were as he replied, "No, I didn't. Maybe they're still on his horse."

The sheriff hollered to one of the other posse members, "Wesley, would you go and check this hombre's horse and see if his saddlebags are still on it."

While Wesley went to check on the saddlebags, the sheriff counted the money he'd removed from the man's pockets.

"There's only a little over three hundred dollars here. Hank said he got away with over five thousand in cold, hard cash. Where do you suppose he hid the rest of the loot," the sheriff said more to himself than to anyone in particular?

"He could have tossed it anywhere along the road, I guess, Ben," Sackett offered.

"Yeah, but it's hard to imagine a man who had just pulled off a successful robbery to just throw the money away like that. No, I think it's around here somewhere."

"We can scour the area and see what we come up with," Sackett said, hoping to sound helpful.

The sheriff looked around at the boot prints that now covered the immediate area. He shook his head as he tried to decipher the different tracks.

"There's no chance of following this guy's footprints, not now. I wish you could have taken him alive, Brent; I really do.

"He didn't leave me any choice, Ben. I fired a warning shot at him and told him to drop his gun and he opened fire on me. I had to take cover and then he fired at me a couple more times and I had to kill him," Sackett said, actually sounding apologetic about the incident.

"I'm not blaming you...I'd have done the same thing. I just meant that if he was alive he could tell us what he did with the money," the sheriff said with a slight grin.

"I know, I know. I was just explaining what happened to you; that's all. I don't like having to kill a man; even an outlaw," Sackett said dropping his head slightly.

"Well, we'll check the area and maybe we can turn up something. We'll also check along the road to make sure he didn't toss the loot somewhere."

Sackett suddenly had another thought. What if he could convince the sheriff that there really wasn't as much money as what they had originally heard? If he could shift the finger of blame towards the freight office manager who had been robbed, he would never have to worry about becoming a suspect.

He'd have to be careful and not overplay his hand, however. He'd keep quiet for the time being, but be ready when the opportunity presented itself. He'd know when the time was right.

The sun was setting low, casting a reddish hue across the landscape, as the posse rode back into Crystal City. The sheriff reined his horse into the hitching rail in front of the sheriff's office while the others, with the exception of Brent Sackett, headed on to their homes.

Having waited for Clay; the man the sheriff had sent for supplies and a buckboard; to return to where the posse had the robber cornered, the sheriff had him take the body to the local undertaker's parlor. Brent followed the sheriff into his office and sat down heavily in a chair.

The sheriff removed his gun belt and hung it on a wall peg next to his desk. He too sat down and cast a long, somewhat hard look towards Sackett. After a few seconds he said what was on his mind.

"It's funny that we didn't find all the money that hombre took from the freight office, don't you think Brent?"

"Yeah, Ben, it is. I've been doing a little thinking on that myself. I say that either he tossed that money somewhere along the way, or, he had an accomplice in the robbery and handed the money off to him. A third possibility is that the freight office manager could be lying about how much the bandit took and is holding a little nest egg for himself," Sackett replied.

The sheriff nodded thoughtfully and then added slowly, "There's one other possibility."

Sackett gave the sheriff a curious look, "Oh, what's that?"

The sheriff paused as he carefully chose his words. "You hid the money before we got to where you'd downed the man."

Sackett bristled, "Is that what you think, Ben? You think I stole the money? Why don't you just say I was in on the robbery from the beginning? After all, that's what you're implying."

"Now, now, I'm just saying that that is a plausible conclusion, that's all. I'm not suggesting you did take the money; but, someone might think that as a possibility," the sheriff quickly added.

"Obviously someone has thought about it already...you! In fact, why don't we go and look in my saddlebags...better still, why don't you search me, Ben. I may have the money stuffed down in my pants, or under my shirt," Sackett said, jumping to his feet.

"Simmer down, Brent; I said it was just a thought. You know how a lawman's mind works. I'm not accusing you, believe me."

"I'm not about to set here and take this...I've had the feeling for sometime that you haven't been pleased with my work as your deputy. You're looking for any excuse to replace me with your brother-in-law, aren't you? I've heard the talk around town."

"I don't know what you heard or who said it, but I wouldn't have Archie as my deputy if he'd do it for free. Who told you that I was looking to replace you? Give me a name."

"I'm not going to involve them in our problem. Ever since you jumped my case about that shooting in the Gold Dust last month you've been on me. Maybe it's time we do part company. After all, two years is a long time on some jobs."

"I don't think we've reached that point, Brent," the sheriff said and then paused as he gave Sackett a questioning look. "Why are you pressing this issue, anyway?"

"Why? You have to ask me why? I'm not going to take the snide remarks and evil eye glances that you've been throwing my way anymore. In fact, I had already been thinking about turning in my badge before this thing today. I guess I was thinking right."

With that, Sackett pulled the badge off his shirt and tossed it on the sheriff's desk. He glared hard at the sheriff; an act that he believed would solidify his statements. The sheriff looked at the badge for a moment and then spoke.

"If that's what you want, okay. I can't see you working as store clerk or teamster though. You're a lawman and I'm the only one for over fifty miles."

"Then I'll go to where there's a need for a lawman. I can do the job of sheriff as well as anyone, and better than most...including you," Sackett snapped.

The sheriff grinned, "That's debatable."

Sackett glared at the sheriff for a moment and then stalked towards the door. Opening it he looked back and spat the words, "Good luck, Sheriff; you'll need it."

2

The sheriff sat and pondered what had just taken place with Sackett. Brent had never shown a tendency towards being temperamental before...why now? The whole scene just didn't seem to sit well with him. It was like eating a big meal and still having a gnawing feeling in the pit of your stomach. Something wasn't right!

Sackett headed down the street for his room at Miss Maude's Boarding House. He had laid the ground work for his exit from Crystal City and his next stop would be where he had hid the money from the freight office robbery.

After packing up his belongings and telling Maude Clarkson that he would be giving up his room and leaving Crystal City, Sackett packed up his horse and rode out of town. He didn't bother to tell any of his friends or acquaintances good-bye; he just rode away.

Making sure that several prominent people saw which direction he left town in, Sackett headed in the opposite direction from where he had hidden the money. He didn't want to give the sheriff or any of the other members of the posse reason to think he knew where the money was and was going back for it. Once he was a safe distance from town he would alter his course and retrieve the stolen loot.

Sackett rode about two miles out of town and then altered his course and began to swing wide around the town of Crystal City. He stayed off the well traveled roads and trails and stuck to riding cross country, thereby lessening the risk of running into anyone who might know him. He kept his horse at an easy lope and covered the distance in short order.

When he reached the spot where they had cornered the bandit, he reined his horse off the road and behind the rock formation. He still wasn't taking any chances of anyone seeing him from the road.

He hurriedly began to throw the brush aside that he'd covered the hollowed out log with and found the stolen money right where he'd left it. A huge smile covered his face as he reached into the log and began to retrieve the four bundles of stolen money.

He stood up to turn and put the money into his saddle bags when he noticed the long shadow of a man standing behind him. Dropping the money, Sackett spun around and went for his gun. He stopped in mid-draw when he saw who it was standing there. It was the sheriff of Crystal City. The sheriff was holding his gun on him.

"Ben...what are you doing here," Sackett asked in a shocked voice?

"I might ask you that same question, Brent. What is that there at your feet? It wouldn't be stolen money would it?"

Sackett's face contorted in anger as he spat out the words, "So what if it is."

"If it is, Brent, you ain't any different than that hombre who stole it from the freight office."

"One thing, though, Ben; I'm a lot better off than he is," Brent said and moved swiftly to his left while drawing his gun.

The sheriff fired a snap shot that winged Sackett in the left shoulder. Sackett was able to get off the next shot that found its mark dead center in the sheriff's chest. The lawman went down hard, but was still alive. The force of the bullet and the searing, burning pain had caused the sheriff to drop his gun.

Sackett walked over to where the sheriff lay and looked down at him. His face wore no expression of guilt, sorrow, or remorse. He stood there staring down at the fallen man with absolutely no emotion whatsoever.

"I hate to do this, Ben, but you leave me no choice," Sackett said as he raised his pistol and cocked the hammer back.

"I thought we were friends, Brent?"

"We were at one time. Things change though, Ben. The War taught me that. I used to be close to my brother, B J, but not anymore."

The sheriff grimaced from the pain in his chest as he spoke, "I thought you said your brother was dead?"

"As far as I'm concerned...he is."

Brent looked at the helpless sheriff and smiled sardonically, "Sorry old hoss," he said and squeezed the trigger, thereby ending the lawman's life.

Brent shook his head as he looked down at the sheriff and slowly dropped the empty cartridges from his .44 caliber Remington revolver. After reloading his pistol he took his neckerchief from around his neck and slipped it under his shirt and over the flesh wound he'd received.

He didn't figure that anyone would find the sheriff's body for several days at least, so didn't try to hide the body. He mounted up and gave one final look at the dead man as he kicked his horse into a trot back towards the road.

"He said he was coming back out here to determine if his suspicions were well founded," Jim Huggins, the only deputy left in Crystal City said as he and two other men looked at the sheriff's corpse. "I guess his suspicions were right," he then added.
"What were his suspicions," Del Wallace asked?
"He said he wondered about the shooting of the old boy who robbed the freight office. He didn't feel right about the whole thing. He thought there was much too much time passed between gunshots after the first one was fired. We could tell that the first shot was fired by a rifle. The bandit had left his rifle in the crevice between the rocks, so the shot had to come from Sackett's gun. It was the time span between that lone rifle shot and the ones from the outlaw's pistol that had him wondering about the whole thing. I don't think he ever accepted Sackett's explanation of the shooting."
"Hey look here," the third man of the trio said. "Here're the empty casings of the gun used to kill Ben."
"Let me see those," the deputy said.
He looked at the casings and shook his head slowly, ".44's. That's what Brent carries; a .44 Remington. I guess we should get the body back to town and get a wire off to the surrounding towns. I'm glad we found Ben's horse. Let's load him up," the deputy said.
The men loaded the sheriff's body across his saddle and they rode back into town. The curious onlookers were stunned when they saw that the dead body belonged to that of Ben Cates, their beloved sheriff. A crowd of people started to follow the men down the street as they rode towards the funeral parlor.

The deputy and the other two men tied up at the hitching rail and began untying the sheriff's body. The undertaker and his helper came out and began to give the men a hand. They carried the body inside and laid it on a table in the back of the parlor.

Looking around the room the deputy gave a slight shudder as he said, "Let's get out of here; this place gives me the willies."

The undertaker; a tall slender man with a chiseled face; grinned as he replied, "You'll all come through here one day."

That was all it took to cause the deputy to hurry back out front with the other two men close behind him. They didn't slow down until they were back at the sheriff's office. The two men went inside with the deputy to discuss business. It looked like he would become the sheriff until a new one could be voted on by the town council.

The deputy shook his head slowly from side to side as the two councilmen explained the situation to him.

"Del, I don't know that I want to be sheriff. I've always been a deputy and that's the Lord's truth. I never really paid that much attention to what Ben did around here. I just concentrated on my job, not his."

"Look Jim, we're just asking you to take the job until we can find the right man to take over. We're not suggesting that you take on the responsibilities of sheriff for good. We may have to send to Laredo or San Antonio for the right man. It shouldn't be over two or three weeks, though. Wouldn't you say so, Arlie?"

"Yeah, three weeks at the most; why, I'll bet you'd make a great substitution until we can find the right man," Arlie Cowan agreed.

"Oh, I guess I could do it. Well, it kind of looks like I ain't got no choice in the matter seeing as how I'm the only deputy left in town. Okay, I'll do it; but only until you can find someone."

"We'll get right on that; and thanks, Jim. This really helps us out. The town can't afford to be without a lawman for long. Uh, do you want to hire a deputy; you can if you think you'll need one," Arlie said.

"Yeah, I'll ask Will Brighton if he would like to sign on as my deputy. He's said several times that he'd like to try his hand at being a lawman."

"Okay, you go ahead and then let us know. Tell him the job pays $30.00 a month plus meals while he's on duty," Del Wallace said.

"Well, I guess my first official act will be sending out telegrams to all the surrounding towns to be on the look out for Brent Sackett. I would imagine he'll head for the border. Once he's across the Rio Grande there ain't a thing we can do about him...ain't that right?"

"That's right. Of course, we could hire a bounty hunter to go after him. They don't give a flip about crossing borders to get their man," Cowan grinned.

"We'd better go and get to work on finding us a new sheriff," Wallace said and he and Cowan got up and headed down the street to the Crystal City Saloon to discuss their next move.

Huggins sat and thought about what Wallace and Cowan had said. He'd go and see if Will Brighton would take the job of deputy, but felt sure he would jump at the chance. Brighton would make a good deputy and even a good sheriff. He was a strong willed man of good character. He'd been married for five years, but was widowed two years earlier.

Huggins got up and grabbed his hat as he headed out the door. He knew where Brighton would be at this time of day. His everyday routine was to go to the Hungry

Heifer Café and have a piece of apple pie and a couple cups of coffee. He had a real weakness for apple pie.

Brighton looked up as Huggins approached him. He grinned as he forked the last piece of apple pie and slipped it into his mouth. Huggins couldn't help but smile at the shear delight he saw on Brighton's face as he savored that last bite of pie.

"Good stuff, ain't it Will," Huggins said as he pulled up a chair and sat down.

"Best stuff on earth…well near to it; anyway," Brighton replied with a grin, and then added, "What brings you in here? I don't think it's the apple pie."

"No, I'm a blackberry man myself. No, this is of a business nature. Will, I have a proposition for you," Huggins started the conversation.

"Oh, does it involve a badge by any chance?"

"Yeah, how'd you know?"

"I saw Cowan and Williams come out of your office. I don't know what the three of you could get your heads together and then you making me a proposition could be except that. Oh, I heard about Ben also. News travels fast around here; and bad news even faster. I'm really sorry."

"Me too; he was a good man."

"Who do you think did it; got any idea?"

"Yeah, I've got a good idea who did it…Brent Sackett."

Brent Sackett rode hard towards Laredo. He wanted to put as much distance as he could between him and Crystal City. Once he arrived in Laredo he would pick up some supplies for his trip into Mexico. With the money he had on him he could live like a king for a number of years down there.

The wound to his shoulder was painful, but it didn't slow him down any; not at first. The constant jarring to the shoulder as he rode along, however, soon forced him to slow his horse to a mere walk. He knew he would need to see a doctor as soon as he got to Laredo.

The slowed pace gave Sackett a chance to lay out a plan of action. He didn't want to stay permanently in Mexico, but that would be the safest place until the heat died down over the killing of the sheriff. He knew that someone would put two and two together and come with him as the prime suspect in the shooting as well as the one who wound up with the freight office's money.

By the time they put all the pieces together, however, his tracks would be stone cold. Heading across the Rio Grande would merely add to the difficulty of following his trail. The doctor who attended to his wound would be the last person to have reason to remember him before he crossed the border into Mexico. That fact, however, could be easily dealt with.

As he laid out his plan he couldn't hold back a grin. He had never envisioned himself as a man on the dodge, but now he was just that...and it didn't bother him in the least. He had always been drawn to excitement and had even hated to see the War end because it called for an end to a life filled with danger. Now he had that same sense of impending doom and seemed to thrive on it.

"Brent Sackett, outlaw," he said aloud and chuckled lowly.

3

At that moment, over two hundred and fifty miles away, another man grimaced with an ache in his shoulder as well. There was nothing really to cause the pain; it just suddenly began to ache. The man flexed slightly and involuntarily moved his hand to his shoulder, wondering what had caused the sudden ache.

"Is something wrong, BJ," Wes Baggett, the top hand on the Sackett ranch asked?

"No, just a sudden ache in my shoulder; it must have been from lifting that calf out of the mud this afternoon," Brian Sackett said to his ranch hand.

"It's probably a case of old age," Wes said with a chuckle.

"Yeah, right; old age at twenty nine," Brian laughed.

"Closer to thirty than you was yesterday," Wes went on.

"I'll start to worry about old age when I reach your years," Brian said to his good friend.

From the kitchen Loretta Sackett called out to her son, "Brian, would you and Wes come in here and give me a hand,"

"Sure thing, Ma," Brian said and he and Wes got up and walked into the large kitchen.

"I want you boys to taste this and tell me if it tastes all right or if I need to throw it out," she said with a slight grin.

BJ and Wes looked at the blackberry cobbler that Mrs. Sackett had made and then towards each other. They couldn't hold back the huge grins that spread over their face as they watched her spoon out two bowls of the still hot dessert.

"I think we're up to the task, aren't we, Wes," BJ stated

"I know I am, but I ain't too sure about you," Wes teased.

"Now I want you boys to tell me the truth. I'm not sure if I put enough sugar in it this time," Loretta said seriously.

"Oh, we'll tell you the truth, but it might take a couple of samplings to really know for sure," Brian said with a wink at Wes.

The two men took the bowl offered them by Mrs. Sackett and held them up to their nose. The aroma caused them both to close their eyes with delight.

"Mm, I can tell you right now that it has plenty of sugar," Wes commented.

They sampled the cobbler and their facial expression said all that was needed; smiles like theirs don't lie. The cobbler was perfect. They began to eat it faster until both bowls were cleaned out.

"Maybe we should make sure the rest of it is as good as this was," BJ said, getting an agreeing nod from Wes.

"I don't think so," Mrs. Sackett said laughingly, "We have to save some for your pa and AJ."

"They don't appreciate the finer things in life like Wes and I do, though, Ma," BJ grinned.

Just then the kitchen door opened and John Sackett and the oldest Sackett boy, AJ, entered the room. John nodded towards Wes, but addressed Brian with a serious look on his face.

"Did you fire Myron Selman this morning, Brian," John asked?

"I did; and with good reason. Did you know he was wanted for killing a man in Abilene on our drive to the railhead," Brian shot back?

"Yes, I knew about it. I was told the man went for his gun first, but Myron beat him to the draw."

"Then we've got two different stories circulating about the shooting. I was told the man called Myron out and when Myron backed down the man turned his back. That's when Myron found the sand to shoot it out with him and shot him in the back," Brian said tightly.

"Who told you that?"

"Tennessee, among others," Brian stated, and then asked, "What did you hear?"

"I heard that the man was caught cheating and Myron called him out. The man went for his gun and Myron shot in self defense."

"And who told you that?"

John paused before answering, "Myron."

"I didn't just go on what Tennessee said on this, Pa. I confirmed it by asking some of the other men who were on that same cattle drive. Two others backed up Tennessee's accounting of the incident. One of them was standing no more than fifteen feet away from Myron when he fired."

"I hate to lose him…he was a good hand," John said with a nod.

"I didn't want us to be harboring a man wanted by the law; should they come looking for him," Brian added.

"No, I wouldn't either. Well, I just wanted to check with you about his firing. Did you pay him off?"

"Yeah, I made a note of it and left it in your ledger over there. He had eighteen dollars and some change coming."

"Okay," John said and noticed Brian rubbing his shoulder area again. "What's wrong with your shoulder?"

"I don't know. It just started aching a few minutes ago. I think I might have strained it when Wes and I pulled that calf out of the mire today. Man, I tell you; that black muck is seeping up in several areas around the ranch. I just hope it doesn't contaminate the water," Brian stated.

"Yeah, I think maybe we should fence those areas off so the cattle don't wander off into it and we wind up losing some of them," AJ agreed.

"I still say that it's old age," Wes said with a wry grin.

AJ looked at Wes and chuckled, "That would be my guess, too."

"When it comes to old age you two would be authorities on the subject, that's for sure," Brian said, getting in the last dig.

John grinned, "I'm glad I have boys older than I am."

The three men laughed at John's remark when there was a knock on the front door. AJ went to see who it was while the others remained in the kitchen.

Suddenly the silence was shattered by the sound of two gunshots. Everyone was stunned for a moment by the unexpected gunfire, but then rushed into the other room to where the shots had been fired. AJ was lying in the threshold of the open front door. He had been shot at close range.

John and Brian stopped to check on AJ's condition, while Wes ran out on the porch to see if he could see who it was who had shot AJ. He heard the sound of hoof beats at the right side of the house and ran to where he could get a look at the rider. He had no trouble identifying the man riding away.

Wes fired a snap shot in the general direction of the fleeing man, but the rider was well out of range of the hand gun. He hurried back to where John, Brian, and Mrs. Sackett were attending to AJ.

"Is he dead," Wes asked?

"No, but it's bad. He's unconscious now. We've got to get a doctor out here, quick. Wes, ride into town and get Doc Adamson; and burn up the road both ways. Did you get a look at who the shooter was?"

"It was Myron Selman. I'd know that Appaloosa and white hat of his anywhere. He told Logan Miller that he was going to head down to San 'Antone' to see that gal friend of his that lives down there. I'll bet that's where he's headed," Wes said hurriedly as he turned and headed out to the hitching rail where his horse was tied.

"Thanks for that, pardner. Now ride hard, Wes; don't waste a second," BJ called after him.

Wes swung into the saddle and gigged his horse into a full gallop. Once Wes had gotten out of sight of the ranch house, he slowed his horse to an easy lope. Since it was over twenty miles into Abilene he didn't want to wind his horse. He figured on hitting a more torrid pace once he neared town to lather up his horse more.

He figured on stopping at the livery stable and grabbing a fresh mount for the ride back. That wouldn't be a problem since the Sackett's owned several businesses in town, including the livery stable. His horse would be well taken care of until he got back into town to return the stable owned horse.

When he reached Abilene, Wes rode up in front of the Ace High Saloon and reined to a stop. Before dismounting he looked down the row of horses tied up out front of the bar. When he saw the lathered buckskin, he grinned. It was only then that he climbed out of the saddle and walked up the four steps to the raised boardwalk. He stopped before entering the saloon and looked up the street towards the doctor's office and saw the doctor's horse and buggy tied up in front. He grinned as he walked on inside the saloon.

Logan Miller was standing at the far end of the bar by himself. When Wes saw him he walked over to where his friend was and slapped him on the back. The two men looked at one another stone faced before suddenly bursting into laughter.

"We pulled that off slicker than a whistle. They fell for the story hook, line, and sinker. Old Myron won't know what hit him when the law comes down on him. His telling you that he was heading for San Antone was a stroke of good fortune. Now we can even blame the missing cattle on him," Wes chuckled as he and Logan spoke of the shooting incident. "What did AJ look like when you dropped the hammer on him?"

"Oh, his eyes widened to about the size of saucers," Logan laughed. "I thought they were going to pop right out of his head."

"I'll kill a little more time before going and fetching the doctor. I can't dilly dally around here too long. You head on back to the ranch from here, but go straight to the big house. I want the Sackett's to see you there. You can mention to them that you saw me burning up the road towards Abilene earlier; but don't forget to play dumb about the shooting," Wes said still grinning.

"Don't worry, pardner, I know my part in this whole thing. You just make sure that AJ doesn't come around and identify me as the shooter. If he does...we'll both swing! And I want to enjoy the money we're going to get for those steers we've been cutting out of the herd," Logan said dropping the grin.

"Yeah, we won't be able to use that black water muck and mire story once they fence those areas off," Wes agreed, and then added, "Let's take that table over there and get away from the bar."

They took a seat away from everybody else and Wes put his feet up on one of the extra chairs to rest his back. The two had another beer and discussed their next move. They kept their conversation strictly between themselves; only including the bartender when they wanted to order another beer. After a couple of beers, they parted company and Wes got up and slowly walked out of the bar while Logan headed back to the Sackett ranch.

The doctor was in his office with a patient when Wes burst through the door. His sudden entrance caused both doctor and patient to jump with a start.

"My Lord, man, are you trying to give us both a heart attack," the doctor yelled.

"Sorry, Doc, but you've got to come quick. AJ Sackett has been shot. He's hurt bad, real bad," Wes said excitedly.

"Okay, have a seat and as soon as I'm finished here, I'll go with you," the doctor said looking from Wes to the young woman sitting across from him.

"What? I'm telling you that AJ is in serious condition. He may not last if you don't come now," Wes demanded.

The doctor looked angrily at the cowhand and then back at the young woman.

"Could you come back tomorrow and let me check this problem out? I can see I'm not going to do a thorough examination today," he said and looked back at Wes.

"Get your bag," Wes said with a frown.

"Okay, okay, hold your horses. I don't want to rush off and forget anything."

The doctor ran his hand across his stubble bearded face as he prepared to address the Sackett family.

"He's in a coma and it's going to be touch and go for the next twenty four to forty eight hours. I can tell you one thing, though; if he pulls through he's going to be limited in what he can do around here for quite some time."

"Just as long as he pulls through, Doc, that's all we want," Loretta Sackett said with a mother's look of concern etched into her pretty face.

"I'll stay here as long as I can; hopefully he'll regain consciousness before too long. The bullets are still in him and I don't want to operate until he comes out of the coma. I can tell you this; it will be a very delicate operation. I take it you can put me up," the doctor said looking from AJ to John?

"We sure can. Loretta will show you to the guest room. It's just down the hall. We usually eat around six o'clock in the evening. If you want anything out of the kitchen before or after then just make yourself at home," John offered.

"Thank you; I usually have a big breakfast, little lunch and light dinner. My stomach won't allow for any more than that," the doctor said.

"Pa, I'll be here until I find out if AJ's going to make it, then I'll be going on a little trip," Brian said more to himself than to the rest of those present.

"Oh, and where might that be," the doctor asked curiously?

"Uh, right now I don't know where that might be. It all depends on where the man who shot AJ is headed. From what Wes Baggett tells me, it will more than likely be San Antonio," Brian said evenly.

"Revenge is never the answer to something like this, Brian. It only leads to more pain and suffering," the doctor said shaking his head.

John interjected his thoughts at that time, "I think we're talking about justice, here, Doc."

"That's why we have lawmen, John. Let them take care of it," the doctor argued.

"I'm not about to let the man who did this get away with it. I'll bring him in to stand trial for his crime...unless he puts up a fight and then I'll kill him wherever it is he decides to make a stand."

"You young people; I'll never understand your reasoning," Doc Adamson said.

"It's not just the young people, Doc. That's the Sackett way. We don't ask anyone to fight our battles for us. We'll take care of it when we can," John stated.

"Doc, I can understand your thoughts on the matter. You take a vow to save lives. I have never taken such a vow," Brian replied.

"You have another law you should abide by, though," the doctor said. "Vengeance is mine, saith the Lord."

"I believe that. But sometimes he uses our hands, eyes, and actions to accomplish it."

"What about 'Though shall not kill?'"

"I haven't killed Selman yet. I'll deal with that law when I have to; but, then Selman didn't pay much attention to that commandment, did he."

"Well, you're going to do what you must. I just hope I don't have to patch either one of you men up. My patient list is full enough as it is."

4

Wes Baggett stood listening to Brian's orders. He wore a solemn look and nodded his head at BJ's words. When Brian had finished giving his list of orders Wes spoke.

"I don't know about this, BJ. Just because the doctor said he thought AJ was out of danger, I don't know that you should be leaving to find Selman. He could take a turn for the worse and how would we be able to contact you?"

"I'll let you know from time to time where I am and you can give me an update on AJ's well being then. I can't let Selman's trail get too cold if I want to catch up to him," Brian said as he adjusted his bedroll in back of his saddle.

"Well I just hope you know what you're doing. Don't forget we have those horses to deliver to the cavalry coming up in a few weeks. You may not even be back for that," Wes pointed out.

"If I'm not then you take care of it. You've seen me handle things enough to know what to do. Whatever you say goes; whatever you say would be just like Pa, AJ or I would say. Pa and I'll back you up one hundred percent. Make sure you check what the going rate for cavalry mounts is and go from there. I'll get in touch with you in a week or so," Brian said as he untied the reins from the hitching rail.

"How're you going to do that? Who knows where you might be in a week," Wes argued?

"Have you ever heard of the telegraph, Wes," Brian grinned as he stepped up on his horse.

"Okay, boss, you win. Don't worry about anything to do with the ranch; I'll keep it running smooth as a Tennessee Walkin' horse," Wes said with a head nod.

"I know you will. I've already said goodbye to Ma and Pa, so I'll say so long to you. I've got a long ride ahead of me; just how long I have no way of knowing. Adios, Amigo," Brian said and reined his horse around and headed out in the direction Selman had taken two days earlier.

Brian (BJ) rode all that day, covering close to fifty miles. Selman had cut cross country which made following his trail a lot easier. The fact that his horse was missing a back shoe added to the ease of following horse and rider. If he should realize it and have another shoe put on it would make tracking him a lot harder.

Seeing as how BJ had worked 'reconnaissance' during the War Between the States, he had become an expert at tracking; as well as other acts associated with that particular field. It was obvious to him that Selman was headed towards San Antonio.

As he rode along he recalled things that Selman had said from time to time, in regards to his past. One of the things BJ remembered was Selman talking about a woman he knew in the small town of Uvalde which wasn't that far from San Antonio. Coupled with what Wes had told him, he figured that Uvalde was Selman's ultimate destination.

It was around nine o'clock in the evening when BJ rode into the small settlement of Coleman. He was tired and dusty and wanted nothing more than a meal, a beer, a hot bath, a close shave, and a soft bed; and in that order. Once he had taken care of those items he would ask around and see if anyone in town might remember seeing a man who fit Selman's description.

Due to the lateness of the hour, Sackett ate before going to the hotel and getting a room. He gave the waitress his order, and then on the outside chance Selman may have eaten there, gave her his description. She was of no help and told him just about half the town fit the man's described.

After dinner BJ went to the hotel where he cleaned up before going next door to the largest saloon in town. He had a beer and asked the bartender the same question he'd asked the waitress. The bartender shook his head no before answering.

"There's a local gunny that might fit the man you described. His name is Johnny Rule. He's mean and always looking for trouble. He's about the same size as the man you're looking for...I hope it's him. I'd like to see this town rid of the man."

"I doubt that it's the same man; but thanks anyway. Just to be on the safe side though, has this Johnny Rule been gone from here for any length of time," Sackett asked?

The bartender shook his head no, "No, I'm sorry to say," and suddenly looked past Sackett.

Sackett grinned at the comment, but didn't notice the look away before answering, "I figure someone will eventually take care of this Johnny Rule."

"Oh, and who might that be....you?

The man's voice from behind Sackett made him turn around. A thin man of about twenty three years of age was standing about six feet in back of Sackett. He stood with his feet apart and his hands hanging over the handles of his two pearl handled pistols.

"What," Sackett asked?

"You said someone would take care of Johnny Rule. I'm asking you if you think you can take me," the man stated.

"I was just making a comment to the bartender," Sackett said and paused, "I take it you're Johnny Rule; is that right?"

Rule nodded his head yes and continued to glare at Sackett, while holding his gunman's pose, "That's right, I'm Johnny Rule. If you think you can 'take care' of me, why don't we find out right here and now."

BJ turned completely around to face the man as he answered, "I'm not looking for you, Rule. I'm looking for a man by the name of Myron Selman."

"You may not be looking for me, but you've found me. Now I'm telling you to go for your gun," Rule said slowly and deliberately.

"I've got no quarrel with you," BJ said evenly.

"No, well I've got one with you. I don't like your looks. And I especially don't like it when total strangers make cockeyed remarks about me," Rule said with a twisted grin.

BJ looked at the bartender and said with a smile, "If this guy doesn't back off, you're about to get your wish."

The bartender grinned, but then looked quickly towards Rule.

"What wish is that, stranger," Rule snapped.

Dropping the smile, Sackett said without hesitation, "To be rid of you once and for all."

Sackett saw Rule's eyes widen as he went for his guns. Both men drew there weapons in a split second, their hand movement being a blur. Two shots rang out semiseriously as the smell of spent gunsmoke hung heavily in the barroom air.

Neither man moved for several seconds, both having appeared to have missed with their shot. Then slowly Johnny Rule's knees began to bend very slowly and he dropped the gun from his hand. As the gun hit the floor, Rule sagged slowly forward and then, he too, fell to the floor...dead.

BJ looked around at the bartender, "You saw it; he forced me to draw down on him."

"I saw it all, and I still don't believe it. You beat Johnny Rule. We're finally rid of the scoundrel," the bartender said and then paused. "But, if I was you I'd hightail it out of here, before the rest of the Rule family hears about it."

Sackett frowned, "Oh?"

"He's got two brothers who are bad too, just not as cantankerous as Johnny. They were close though; but the old man...he's the worst of the lot," the bartender warned.

"I'll be leaving in the morning," Sackett said.

"Then I won't send a rider out to their ranch until then. They live about eight or nine miles out of town. That should give you a good head start," the bartender said thoughtfully.

"What do you mean 'I won't send someone out to their ranch'? Why should you have to do it; isn't that the sheriff's job," BJ asked?

"I am the sheriff," the man said with a grin. "I was an eyewitness to the goings on here."

"I guess I lucked out there, then. Who's going to question the town sheriff?"

"No one around these parts; not where getting rid of Johnny Rule is involved; well, no one other than the Rules, that is;. You did this town a favor. It's just like I said though; you didn't do your self a lot of good by killing him."

"I like that better than the alternative; I can tell you that," Sackett said, drawing a belly laugh from the sheriff. "I'll be in my room if you need me, Sheriff," Sackett said and headed for his hotel room.

The next morning BJ arose early to hit the trail. He went down to the desk clerk to pay his bill and saw six people, three men and three women, seated in the small lobby. As he approached the front desk one of the men stood up and timidly approached him.

"Excuse me, sir, but we'd like to speak with you if we may," the man asked?

BJ looked at the man and then at the others who stood up also and moved slightly towards him.

"Yeah, sure," BJ said.

"I take it you are the man who...," he paused as if looking for the right word, "uh...killed...Johnny Rule," the man who appeared to be the spokesman asked?

"I'm afraid so. Who might you be," Sackett asked?

"I am the mayor here. Actually I appointed myself to the office since the town didn't have one and no one wanted to run for the office."

"They must like you, you're still mayor," Sackett grinned.

"I suppose so, now that I think about it," the man said, also smiling at the thought. "What I, uh, we wanted to do was thank you for freeing our town from the hold that Johnny Rule held over us. You'll never know what an evil man he is...uh...was."

"I didn't know the man and didn't come here looking for trouble. He forced the issue, and from what I hear, had done it before. I take no pleasure in killing a man, any man, but sometimes it can't be avoided. This was one of those times. Since I had to take another's life, I'm just glad it was someone like this Johnny Rule," Sackett said evenly.

"If you would be interested in being our sheriff we would sure be appreciative," the mayor said still smiling.

"No, I'm leaving and need to get a move on. Thanks for the offer, but I'm a rancher, not a lawman."

"Well, like I said, we just wanted to let you know how much we appreciate what you did for our town," the mayor said extending a hand towards the other five people, who moved closer.

BJ smiled and nodded as he looked from the mayor towards the other folks. With that, each person moved up and shook his hand, expressing their gratitude. BJ couldn't help but wonder just what kind of a man he had done away with, anyway. Obviously the man had terrorized the entire community.

After saying goodbye, BJ went to the livery stable where he'd left his horse and saddled up. He had stayed an hour or so longer than he'd wanted to, but the rest had done him good. His conscience was also soothed at the knowledge of ridding the town of someone like Rule. Still, he didn't like the feeling that killing brought with it.

As luck would have it, BJ picked up Myron Selman's horse's hoof prints again within a mile of the city limit sign. He knew he was right about where Selman was more than likely headed. The time seemed to pass by more quickly, especially since he had time to do some thinking about the entire situation in which he now found himself.

5

Brent Sackett rode down the dimly lit, narrow main street of Encinal just after midnight. The only place open at that time of the night was one small, dimly lit saloon. He tied up in front of the sign that merely read, 'Bar', and went inside. He found a small, rickety table in the back and plopped down in the chair.

A plump, but pretty Mexican woman with one side of her cream colored blouse pulled down over one shoulder came over and looked at the haggard looking stranger in town. Her English was good, but she still carried an accent.

"So what would you like," she said with wry smile?

"A doctor...you wouldn't have one handy would you," Brent said forcing a grin of his own.

"Oh, you are hurt," the woman said as she noticed the blood stain for the first time.

"It ain't much, but it does pain me a little," Brent replied.

"I will get you the doctor," the woman said and started to leave.

"Where are you going to find a doctor at this time of night," Brent wanted to know?

"He's right over there," she said and motioned towards a man wearing a black coat with his head resting on a table top. "The one with the black coat," she called back to him.

Brent smiled to himself as he watched the woman approach the doctor. She gently shook the doctor, and after a couple of attempts was able to rouse him. He listened to the woman for a moment then looked over towards Sackett. He nodded his head yes, and said something to the woman that Sackett could not hear, but figured the doctor had said he would check the man out.

The woman turned and looked at Sackett and nodded yes, and then made a motion as if to ask if he wanted something to drink. Sackett nodded and held up his thumb and forefinger to indicate he wanted a double shot of whiskey. She walked to the bar and placed the order.

The bartender looked towards Sackett and then poured two double shots. The woman picked up the two drinks and carried them back to where Sackett was sitting. She placed the two drinks on the table and then sat down.

"Did I ask you to join me," Sackett asked stern faced?

The woman frowned at the remark and then responded, "You didn't tell me not to."

Sackett grinned at her answer, "Have a seat."

The woman smiled as she realized he was only teasing her. She picked up the shot glass and leaned back in the chair.

"Where are you from," she asked?

"Here and there...no where in particular," Sackett replied.

"Where are you headed," she went on?

"I'm here now...and that's what's important ain't it?"

"Fortunate for me, I think."

"And me, right?"

"Si...and you," she smiled showing even, white teeth.

"When did that doctor say he'd take a look at my shoulder?"

She looked back towards the doctor and then back at the handsome stranger, "Right now."

"Is he sober enough to attend to anyone?"

"That is his usual condition, so I think maybe so."

Sackett looked and saw that the doctor had gotten up from his chair and was making his way over to where he and the woman were seated.

Walking up to the table the doctor asked in a slightly slurred voice, "What seems to be the problem, young man?"

"I got a slight wound to my shoulder, Doc," Sackett replied.

"Hmm, let me take a look at it. Take off your shirt."

"Here," Brent asked?

"What's wrong with that? It saves us a trip down the street to my office. Open up your shirt," the doctor ordered.

"No modesty around here, I can see," Sackett said with a frown.

"I didn't ask you to remove your pants, son," the doctor replied evenly. "I doubt that Carmen would have been embarrassed if I had and you did...remove your pants, that is."

The woman grinned at the doctor's comment and gave Brent a knowing look. He returned her gaze and smiled. Opening his shirt Brent did a double take as the doctor's face drew near enough to his for him to smell the strong odor of whiskey on the doctor's breath.

"Are you up to this," Brent asked?

"What makes you ask a foolish question like that? Oh, you mean the whiskey...it steadies my nerves."

Carmen grinned at the doctor's words and added, "Sometimes he gets so steady he can't even move."

"Now, now, Chiquita, be nice," the doctor said as he looked closely at Sackett's wound. "Hmm, this doesn't look too bad. So how'd you get a gunshot wound, anyway?"

"I was hunting with a friend and he accidentally shot me," Sackett lied.

"Oh, is that right? What were you hunting?"

"What difference does that make? Rabbits," Sackett said, hoping to bring an end to the questioning.

"Rabbits, huh; well this is certainly the area for that. If you like Jack Rabbits that is," the doctor then added.

"Maybe I do."

"Let me get my bag; it's over by the bar," the doctor said and gave Sackett a long look.

He turned and walked to the end of the bar where he'd left his black bag, probably before he had needed to take a table where he had been seated. Sackett watched him very closely, never taking his eyes off the man. The doctor picket up the small black medical bag and said something to one of three men who were playing cards at one of the tables. Sackett couldn't hear if anything had been said, but he definitely had the feeling the doctor had said something to one of the men. He was right.

The doctor walked back to where Sackett and Carmen were sitting. Just after he got there and opened his bag the man he'd spoken to got up and started walking their way. Sackett watched the man as he approached. When the man was about ten feet from the table, Sackett saw the badge under the man's vest. Sackett slowly moved his hand towards his holstered pistol.

"Howdy; new in town ain't ya'," the sheriff asked?

Sackett nodded his head in the affirmative as he replied, "Yeah, I'm just passing through."

"The doc here says you have a gunshot wound to the shoulder. He said it was a hunting accident...is that right?"

"That's what I told him all right. Rabbits," Sackett said seriously.

"Rabbits, huh? Where did this...accident, happen?"

"Up north about fifteen miles," Sackett said looking from the sheriff to the doctor who had started attending to the shoulder.

"Where's your friend now," the sheriff asked?

"I don't know. He headed back home I guess. He ain't with me if that's what you're getting at," Sackett said attempting to disarm the sheriff's questioning.

"So he shot you and then just let you strike out on your own to find a doctor, is that it? Not a very good friend, I'd say," the sheriff said as he stood in front of Sackett with his thumbs tucked under his belt buckle.

Sackett was getting tired of the questioning so decided to bring it to a halt.

"That was my feelings exactly, Sheriff. I won't be seeing the man again. He was more interested in getting back to his woman than he was about my well being. Accidents happen and that's exactly what this was...an accident. It was also an accident that taught me a very valuable lesson. Know as much as you possibly can about a friend if you decide to go hunting with them. Be it rabbit, deer, elk, antelope, or bear."

The sheriff nodded his head slightly and then cocked it to one side as he asked his next question.

"Where'd you come from?"

"San Antonio...and I'm headed for Rio Grande City."

Just then the doctor probed a little too hard which caused Brent to flinch.

"Hold still, young man," the doctor snapped.

"I will if you stop poking me," Brent replied.

"I have to find out if that bullet is still in there," the doctor said continuing to probe.

"Hmph...that really does smart, Doc! Ain't you got anything to deaden the pain?"

"Oh, yeah; here take a shot of this," the doctor said grabbing the bottle that Brent had bought and shoving it towards his patient.

After Brent took a long swig from the bottle he handed it back to the doctor who took a long drink also.

Brent looked questioningly at the man attending him, "I hope you know what you're doing," he said seriously.

"I'm not going to hurt you as much as the man who shot you did," the doctor answered back.

The sheriff held a steady gaze on Brent, finally speaking his mind, "I want to know why anyone would go rabbit hunting in these parts. That makes no sense whatsoever."

Sackett bristled, "Look, my friend and I were on our way to Rio Grande City and needed food. We went out in some brush because we saw a rabbit and tried to hem it in. The rabbit started running and my friend didn't know I was in back of a thicket. The bullet hit me. He finally said he was going back home and left. That's all there is to it."

"I just want to make sure you didn't take out a little revenge on your friend for shooting you. You didn't, did you," the sheriff asked?

"I'm only going to say this one more time, Sheriff...Oww...there you go again, Doc."

"Sorry."

Sackett went on, "My friend, Joe Smith, went back home to San Antonio because he missed the woman he had been living with. Now you have a name and a town, so go and check it out. I'm on my way to Rio Grande City and I'm not going to talk about it anymore."

The sheriff glared at Sackett, but didn't offer a comeback immediately. After a few seconds, however, he asked, "I suppose you have the money to pay the doc here for his services...you do don't you?"

"Yeah, I've got money to pay the doc. Why do you ask?"

"We have a vagrancy law here in Encinal. If you ain't got no money, we don't want you in our town."

"Like I said, I've got money and I don't want to spend anymore time in your one horse town than I have to, believe me. As soon as the doctor patches me up I'll be on my way."

"How long do you think you'll be, Doc," the sheriff asked?

"Not long; it looks like the bullet passed clean through without hitting anything serious. No fragments left behind that I can find."

"You've got one hour from the time the doc finishes with you, and then I want you out of my town," the sheriff said in a low, menacing voice.

"Thanks, I won't need that much time," Brent replied.

"One hour," the sheriff repeated as he started to leave.

"I'll stop by and say goodbye, Sheriff," Sackett said with a crooked grin.

"No need for that, just make sure you're gone and that will be all I need," the sheriff said and walked out.

Brent watched the sheriff leave as a deep set frown came to his face which seemed to cause a veil of darkness to cover his eyes. The doctor noticed and literally shied away from his patient for a moment. The room seemed to lose some of its warmth as if the Grim Reaper had just entered the room.

"Well, I'm done here, sir," the doctor said.

"How much do I owe you, Doc," Sackett asked?

"How about twenty dollars," the doctor replied?

Brent looked at him and gave a smirk, "Working cowhands have to work a month to make that kind of money," he said.

"Working cowboys didn't take the time, effort, and money to go to school to learn doctoring skills, either did they," the doctor said firmly.

"Did you," Brent asked seriously?

The doctor didn't answer right away which seemed to say a lot about the qualifications of the man.

"Here," Brent said and fished a twenty dollar gold piece out of his pocket.

"Thank you my good man," the doctor said and started to leave.

"Hey, wait a minute. I want something to put on this wound when I change the bandages. You know, a salve or something," Brent said.

"Oh, yeah, I can take care of that," the doctor said and pulled a jar of ointment out of his bag and handed it to Brent.

"Thanks, Doc," Brent said.

Buttoning up his shirt again, Brent took one more shot of whiskey and then put the cork back in the bottle. Getting up slowly, he walked over to the bar and asked the bartender a question.

"Where is the sheriff's office from here," he asked?

"Oh, it is about five doors down, but on the other side of the street. You can see the sign from out in front of this place."

"Thanks," Brent said as he turned and headed for the door.

He walked out onto the boardwalk and looked down the street towards the sheriff's office. A grin tugged at the corner of his mouth as he untied his bridle reins from the hitching rail. He mounted up and rode down the street to the sheriff's office where he stopped and looked through the shade drawn window. When he saw the silhouette of the sheriff pass by the window, he stepped down off his mount.

Still holding the crooked grin on his face, Brent opened the sheriff's office door and looked in. The sheriff had his back turned towards him and didn't hear the door open. Sackett waited until the sheriff turned around; when he did the lawman's eyes widened.

"I'm leaving now, Sheriff, but I wanted to leave something for you and your town to remember me by," Sackett said evenly.

"Oh, and what's that?"

"This," Sackett said and drew his pistol!

The sheriff went for his gun, only then realizing he had removed his gun belt when he had entered the office earlier. His eyes darted from Sackett to the wall peg where he had hung his gun belt, then back towards Brent.

The sound of the hammer being cocked seemed to fill the silent room. The sheriff swallowed hard, his Adam's apple dancing in his throat. The tightening of Sackett's finger on the trigger as he slowly squeezed it had not escaped the sheriff's attention.

Suddenly the room exploded in a loud clap of gunfire. The bullet found its mark in the sheriff's chest, knocking him back against the wall. He looked down at the front of his shirt and saw the spurt of blood just before he began to slowly slump to the floor. A trail of blood was left smeared down the wall as the mortally wounded sheriff slid to the floor.

Brent stood there for a moment merely staring at the dead lawman. Then, almost as if slapped to awareness, he turned and rushed out to his horse. He mounted up and kicked the horse into an easy gallop out of town. Brent Sackett was developing a gunman's taste for blood.

6

The sheriff of Laredo sat in his office with his feet up on his desk. An old Mexican man stood in front of the sheriff's desk holding a beat up old straw hat in his hands. The sheriff looked at the old man and took a bite of his nearly over ripe peach; the juice ran off his chin and dripped down onto his shirt front.

"Sheriff, you have my son in jail because he was drunk, but my son does not even drink. He suffers from an illness that causes him to act drunk at times. We do not know what causes this but when he eats something sweet he seems to get a little better."

"I don't know anything about that, Alejandro; I only know that he was lying in front of the saloon over there, out of his head, mumbling something that I sure couldn't understand. I figured he got him a bottle of Tequila and downed it. I'll let him sleep it off and then cut him loose. I want you to keep him out of town though until you find out what it is that causes him to act like he does. He might be carrying some kind of rare disease or something."

With the front door of the sheriff's office open he was able to see anyone who might be riding past his office down Laredo's main street. Just then he noticed a man who obviously had been on the trail for several days, pass by. He could tell by the white, chalk like dust that covered the man. The sheriff got up from his chair and walked past Alejandro Reyes to the open door.

"Hmm, stranger in town," the sheriff said to himself.

"Por favor," Mr. Reyes asked?

"Oh, it was nothing. Listen, Mr. Reyes, if you'll take your son home with you I'll let him go now. You keep him out of town though, unless you come in with him, do you hear me?"

"Oh si, si Sheriff, I will do that."

The sheriff stepped out onto the boardwalk in front of the office and watched the stranger. The man tied up at the Laredo House, the best hotel the town had to offer. He'd make it a point to find out a little about the stranger in town, but that would have to wait for the time being.

He stepped back inside and went to the cell and opened the door. The young man lay on the narrow cot against the back wall of the cell. The sheriff kicked the cot, shaking it in the process.

"Okay, get up Miguel," he called out in a loud voice.

The boy didn't move, which brought another kick from the sheriff. Still the boy didn't move.

"Come on, get up," the sheriff snapped angrily, "Your pa is here to take you home."

When the boy didn't move again, the sheriff shook him by the shoulder. The sixteen year old still didn't move.

"Get up, son," the sheriff said with some concern showing in his tone of voice.

Mr. Reyes stood in back of the sheriff with a worried look on his face. The sheriff continued to try and rouse the boy until it was obvious he was not responding. That was what prompted the sheriff to take the young man's pulse. After feeling for a pulse and not finding one, he put his ear to the boy's chest in search of a heart beat. He slowly turned and looked at the boy's father.

"Mr. Reyes, I'm afraid your son is dead. I can't find a pulse or a heart beat. I'm sorry," the sheriff said with a pained look.

"Dead...my Miguel is dead," Senor Reyes said in a stunned voice.

"Whatever caused him to act drunk must have been serious enough to kill him," the sheriff said as he stepped to one side and allowed the boys father to move up to where his son lay.

Mr. Reyes knelt down by the small cot and took his son's hand. He too felt for a pulse, but could not find one. He looked helplessly up at the sheriff and then back at the face of his boy.

"Miguelito...oh, my Miguelito," the boy's grief stricken father said as tears filled his eyes.

"I'll have the undertaker come over and take care of his body if you'd like me to, Alejandro," the sheriff said firmly.

Senor Reyes gave the sheriff a hard look and then said, "I will take care of my son's body."

"It's no trouble, I can assure you," the sheriff said somewhat insistently.

"He is my son; I will take care of him," Alejandro said with finality in his voice.

"If you insist. I'll need this cell, though."

"I will have him out of here in five minutes," Senor Reyes said angrily and turned and walked out of the sheriff's office.

The sheriff watched as the elderly man departed. He shook his head slowly and said to himself, "I'll never understand some people. Here I go and offer to take care of things and what does he do? He acts like it's my fault his son died."

Earl Rule held the black leather Bible over his head and cried out in a loud, booming voice, "An eye for an eye and a tooth for a tooth. This man of evil took the life of Johnny and I shall have the life of this servant of Satan, or my name is not Earl Alonso Rule. I want you boys to get your guns and pack some grub. We're going to find this man and see to it that he dies in the same manner as Johnny."

"Pa we don't even know this man's name," Cory Rule, the eldest of the Rule brothers, said.

"We'll find out what his name is, Cory. I want you and Rupert to go into town and talk to everyone you can about his man. Someone knows something about him. If he's from these parts we'll find him. We owe him," Earl said as he slammed the Bible down on the table top.

"When do you want us to go, Pa," Cory asked?

"Now...get a move on. I don't want the trail to grow ice cold."

"Okay, Pa, right away," Cory said and then added, "Come on, Rupert...you heard what Pa said."

The Rule family took pride in living up to their name and would do anything to hold rule over the community with which they chose to do business; they preferred ruling it by fear rather than respect, however.

The Rules covered the distance between their ranch and the town of Coleman without so much as a word between them. Earl Rule contemplated what he would do to 'loosen the tongue' of anyone in town that might know something about the shooting of Johnny.

Johnny Rule had always been Earl's favorite son because Johnny reminded his father of him. Earl had been a real hell raiser in his younger days, but had somehow escaped the same fate handed to his boy. As the three of the men rode, Earl thought of many things associated with his son. One of the most prevalent thoughts was the last warning he had issued Johnny the day he was gunned down. He had told Johnny to get the chip off his shoulder that he'd carried with him from breakfast that morning, or it might get him in a passel of trouble. Johnny hadn't heeded his warning and now he was dead.

Cory was the smarter of the Rule boys, but played it down when around his pa. He saved his wisdom for his poker playing pals. They saw an entirely different side of him than the one he presented to Earl. It was partly due to the fact that Earl's violent temper was enough to intimidate both boys.

Rupert was the quietest of the three Rule boys. He was a deep thinker that his mother still looked at as her baby. Rupert was one of those 'still waters runs deep' personalities that caused everyone to wonder what he was all about. Earl had quit trying to figure his boys out long ago and figured it was easier to rule them with an iron fist. Rupert had certainly inherited his father's explosive temper, however.

When the Rule's reached the town of Coleman, they headed straight for the sheriff's office; the first man Earl wanted to question was the sheriff. The second place they would look for answers would be the saloon where Johnny had been killed. That was where Earl figured he'd get more details surrounding his son's death.

"Now you're going to tell me everything you can about this good for nothing who murdered my boy," Earl demanded of the sheriff.

"I told you I do not have any idea who the man was, Earl. He came in, had a couple of straight whiskey shots and started to leave. Johnny prodded him; prodded him hard; and then Johnny went for his gun. The stranger beat him to the draw and you know the rest," the sheriff said evenly.

"Did you see the gunfight?"

"Yeah, I stood right over there and watched the entire thing. He was just a hair faster than Johnny," the bartender stated.

"You watched him gun down my boy and did nothing," Earl said, his face reddening as his anger boiled inside him.

"Earl, Johnny started the whole incident. I couldn't arrest the man for merely defending himself," the sheriff said with a deep frown.

"No one was faster than my boy with a six gun. He wasn't that good with a long gun, but he could handle a six shooter better than anyone I've ever seen. Now tell me all you know about this varmint that killed him," Earl demanded.

"I can't tell you something I don't know. If you want to ask around go ahead, but there weren't very many customers in here when the shooting took place," the sheriff replied.

Earl looked around the barroom and raised his voice to a level that everyone could hear him quite plain.

"Listen up. I'm looking for the man who gunned down my son, Johnny, in cold blood. Now if you'll come over and tell my sons and me what you know we'll certainly remember you for it," Earl coaxed, and then threatened, "And if you know something and don't tell us, we'll remember you for that, too."

No one came forward which drew a stream of curse words from Earl. He and his boys stormed out of the saloon and headed for the funeral parlor to view the body. When they were escorted to the viewing room, Earl removed his hat, but his boys didn't. When he noticed their disrespect he turned and began to hit both boys with his hat.

"Don't you have any respect for the dead? That's your brother lying in there," Earl yelled out angrily as the boys covered up to avoid getting hit in the face by their pa flailing his hat.

They quickly pulled their hats off and held them in front of them once he stopped hitting them.

"There...that's better," Earl said as he glared at them.

Earl looked straight ahead as he and his sons entered the room that held Johnny's dead body. Cory and Rupert, however, looked at everything except the pine box that held their brother.

As they walked up next to the body, Earl looked down to hide the fact that he had tears in his eyes. When the boys looked at Johnny's body, Cory grinned.

"Why that's the best I've seen Johnny look in years," he said, his comment getting a nod from Rupert.

Earl didn't respond to Cory's comment other than slowly turning his head and giving him a hard glare. The two boys quickly dropped the grins from their face. The three of them stood there for several minutes, not speaking; Earl simply holding his hat in his hand with his head bowed. Cory and Rupert kept their heads down most of the time, but would raise them just long enough to see what their pa was doing.

Finally Earl straightened up and with a stern look on his face, turned and strode steadily out of the room. His two sons followed him. Once outside Earl put his hat on as they walked to where their horses were tied.

When they reached their mounts, Earl slipped the leather loop of his quirt handle off from around the saddle horn. Suddenly he whirled around and violently began to whip his two sons for the disrespectful comment they had shown their dead brother.

"You good for nothing whelps; I'll teach you to show a little more respect for the dead. That was your blood kin layin' back there and you acted like it was just some useless waddy. Now get on those horses and go get us a room. We ain't leaving here until we find out who it was that killed Johnny," he growled as he finally stopped the whipping of his two sons.

"Okay, Pa, we're sorry. We want to see the man who did this pay for it just as much as you," Cory called back as he and Rupert hurried towards the hotel.

7

BJ Sackett reined his horse to a halt when he reached the fork in the trail and a sign post that gave the mileage to several different towns. It had been two and a half days since he'd been forced to kill Johnny Rule, but the thought of it still bothered him.

The sign post read Fredericksburg 10 miles; San Antonio 80 miles. He felt he was gaining on Myron Selman although he had not been able to pick up Selman's horse's hoof prints for quite a ways. He still felt sure that the man who had shot his brother was headed for San Antonio and the woman he'd spoken of so often.

BJ patted his horse's neck and spoke softly to the lathered animal.

"It won't be long, boy. You'll get a good rest tonight and a belly full of oats. Fredericksburg is only ten miles away."

The horse shook its head up and down, as if wanting to move on. The spirited animal seemed to be able to travel at a gentle lope all day long and not tire. Still, Brian held the horse in check, forcing it to take a breather.

As he sat there looking around the surrounding area, a barred wagon topped a slight rise to the east. There were two men aboard and both wore badges on their vests. When they got within earshot Brian greeted them.

"Howdy, you must have just delivered or are going after a prisoner or two," he said with a smile.

"Goin' to get 'em; and it's three," the driver of the prisoner wagon replied. "Whoa, mules," he then called out to the team.

"Where do you have to go to get them," Brian asked?

"San Angelo. The sheriff there is holding three men who robbed the Texas Cattleman's Bank in San Marcos. Where are you headed," the driver asked?

"San Antonio; I'm tracking a man who shot my brother. I'm sure that's where he's headed," BJ said honestly.

"I don't see a badge," the man siding the driver stated.

"No, I'm not a lawman. I plan on taking him back to stand trial for the shooting though," BJ said honestly.

The two lawmen looked quickly at one another and then back at Sackett.

"I hope you're not planning on taking the law into your own hands," the driver said.

"If bringing a man in to stand trial is taking the law into my own hands, then I guess that's exactly what I'll be doing. I'm not going after him to kill him, if that's what you mean...unless he forces it, that is," BJ said firmly.

"What line of business are you in, pardner," the driver asked?

"Rancher; just out of Abilene; why," BJ questioned?

"I've never known a cowhand to be handy with a six gun. I hope you don't go off and get yourself shot up," the driver replied.

"I can handle a six gun as well as most lawmen, I'm sure," BJ said with confidence.

"I know, you can hit a target at fifty paces; but that target isn't shooting back at you," the driver said.

"I've had targets that have shot back; an entire army," BJ grinned.

"War, huh," the driver said with a nod.

"Yep, afraid so; it's not something I like to dwell on, but we all fell on one side or the other."

"I won't ask which side you were on. No sense in discussing it now, anyway," the driver said.

"I'll ask though," the deputy asked.

"The North...I'm certainly not ashamed of it."

"A Yankee; I should have guess it," the deputy said with a smirk.

"Back off Chester," the driver of the wagon said quietly.

"I had a brother that fought for the South. He was killed. Did you lose any kin in the War," BJ asked with a frown?

"Yeah, I lost a couple of kinfolk."

"I'm sorry to hear it. Let's hope we never have another war like that," BJ said lessening the frown.

"I doubt we'll ever see one," the driver replied.

BJ nodded and shifted in the saddle, "Well, I'd better get a move on. I wish you fellas a safe journey."

"Thanks, same to you," the driver said.

BJ kicked his horse up and headed on his way. The War wounds were still evident even after six years since the surrender. The talk of the War caused BJ to recall a number of things that he'd tried hard to put out of his memory. He was usually successful during the daylight hours, but he couldn't control his nightly dreams.

As he rode along the thought of one battle he'd been involved in kept trying to force its way to the front of his thought process. Because of his fatigue he began to slip back to that day seven years before.

Brian's commanding officer gave the order for them to attack a Southern stronghold. The Northern army was walking straight into cannon fire and Southern sharp shooters who were dug into a steep hillside. Men were falling on both sides of BJ as they raced up that blasted hill.

A cannon blast a few yards away from BJ knocked him to the ground. He was disoriented and for a second had absolutely no idea where he was at. When he regained his sensibilities he thought he had been blinded; there was a heavy pressure on his forehead and he couldn't see.

He began to struggle to relieve the heaviness that seemed to have him penned down. What he felt was two dead bodies lying atop him. Once he managed to extricate himself he saw that one of the men had no head. When the shock of the tragedy hit him, he threw up what little he'd had to eat that day. The man with the missing head was BJ's seventeen year old friend he had made the first day he arrived in camp.

Suddenly and violently Sackett's head jerked as if someone had slapped his face. He returned to the present and immediately got his mind on something else. Still, when he closed his eyes, he could actually see the event like it had just happened that day.

Softly BJ began to sing a song he'd learned from his Ma. The song was one of his mother's favorite songs, "Red River Valley." The words were somewhat sad, yet comforting at the same time.

"Come and sit by my side, if you love me; do not hasten to bid me adieu; but remember the Red River Valley, and the cowboy who loved you so true," BJ sang as he rode along.

After singing the song over and over, he changed the tune to another of his mother's favorites; Aura Lee. After singing it several times he tired of it and turned his full attention to the trail ahead.

BJ topped a small ridge and pulled his mount to a halt. Off to his right and atop a parallel ridge four Kiowa Indians appeared. They all four were looking towards him. Movement on his left caused him to look in that direction. Three more Kiowa topped a slight ridge there as well.

BJ hadn't heard of any Indian trouble from any of the folks he'd met along the way. Seeing seven Kiowa together seemed like more than just a hunting party. They weren't close enough to see if they were wearing war paint or not, but BJ wasn't about to take any chances.

He started to turn his horse around, but thought better of it. He had heard that a ploy of the Kiowa was to get one of their intended victims to do just that. The sight of several braves would make retreating the most logical thing for a person to do. Once the victim reversed direction he would then be faced with several more braves who stayed out of sight when the victim had passed by them originally. Their victim would be boxed in with no hope of escape.

BJ kicked his horse into a full run in the same direction he'd been heading. His move caught the small war party by surprise, but they quickly gave chase. Fortunately, there was a small steep banked creek on the side of the trail of the four Kiowa braves, which would not allow them to cross at an intersect point where they would be able to cut him off.

The Indians on the other side of the trail were a little farther away from him, so they would not be able to block his way either. At least he had an avenue of escape; as long as there weren't more braves ahead, that is.

The big dappled grey that BJ was riding seemed to sense the urgency of the moment. His strides were long, his speed unmatched by the smaller Indian ponies. BJ was able to put some distance between he and his pursuers. The Indians did not fire any shots at the fleeing Sackett, but he knew a couple of them were carrying rifles.

The thought crossed his mind that perhaps they were just playing a little mind game with him. He'd heard that sometimes the younger braves would make sport out of chasing a lone traveler. He couldn't take the chance of thinking in those terms, however. If he was wrong it would be all over but the scalping.

Hopefully he would meet up with someone heading the other way that could help him fend off the Indians. That was a thought that was soon dispelled, however, when he topped a slight rise that allowed him to see a ways down the trail. He didn't see any other travelers approaching; more importantly, however, he didn't see any more Kiowa either.

The grey began to put more distance between them and their pursuers. It was only when the Indians realized this that the first shot was fired. The bullet came close enough to BJ for him to hear its buzz as it cut through the warm Texas air. He leaned a little more out over the horse's neck to make himself a smaller target, now that they had begun firing at him.

A simple stroke of the neck was all the urging the big grey needed to keep the torrid pace he was setting. The smaller Indian ponies could not keep up and soon the Indians were out of rifle range. Sackett knew, however, his fiery mount could not maintain that kind of speed for long. He began to look for a place to hole up and let the Indians pass by. It wasn't long before he saw just such a spot.

Off to his right BJ saw an outcropping of rocks on a ridge that would make a good spot to make a stand. If he could leave the road without providing an easy trail to

Across the Rio Grande

follow he could take cover in the rocks and hopefully the Indians would not find that he had circled back on them. Again, he saw what he needed.

There was a small grove of trees at the end of a small draw to his right. On the other side of the trees was the lower end of the ridge that held the rock outcropping. A quick look back over his shoulder told him that his pursuers were just making their descent down into a low spot in the road. He just might be able to make it to the grove of trees before they topped the rise.

He reined the grey off the road and cut across to the grove of cottonwoods. Once there he kept up the pace through the grove and up the ridge on the other side. To his good luck, he had topped the ridge and was over it before the Indians reached a spot that allowed them to see him.

He circled back to the rocky point and reined his horse to a halt. He could feel the deep breathing action of the grey as it pranced around, pawing the ground as if wanting to keep running. He couldn't hold back the smile at the heart the animal showed.

Sackett climbed off the grey and after wrapping the reins around a small boulder, grabbed his Winchester. He hurried into the rocks to a point that would allow him a good view of the surrounding area. He could see the grove of trees as well as the road beyond them. He could also see the small Kiowa war party.

The band of Kiowa rode past the grove of trees without noticing that he had veered away from the road. Suddenly they pulled their ponies to a skidding halt. Sackett watched as they turned around and headed back up the road in the direction from which they had come...but why?

At first he thought maybe they had realized he had cut off the road. That thought was short lived, however. A cavalry detail suddenly appeared over the crest of the hill and had given chase to the Kiowa war party. BJ grinned at his good fortune, but the grin faded quickly.

About half of the war party stayed on the road, but the other six members decided to head for the outcropping of rocks where Sackett had hidden. BJ got ready to open fire on them when they got within range.

He took aim at the lead member of the band heading directly at him. He slowly cocked the hammer back on the rifle.

"Keep coming," he said softly as he took a fine bead on the Indian.

When the Indians drew to about one hundred and fifty yards, Sackett squeezed off the first round from his long gun. The Indian did a backwards somersault off the back of his horse. The other six members of the band slowed momentarily, but continued to ride towards the rocks.

Sackett ejected the empty while jacking another shell in the chamber. Another shot and another Kiowa hit the ground. The other four began firing blindly towards the rocks, the bullets ricocheting off the rocks near where Sackett was positioned, but never coming very close to him.

Another well aimed shot and another Kiowa fell from his horse. That was all it took to veer the other three Indians away from the rocks and back towards the road. They rode parallel with the road until they were beyond the cluster of rocks, then they went over the ridge and down the other side, away from the road.

The cavalry detail continued to pursue the ones who had stayed on the road. They were out of Sackett's view, but he could hear rifle fire. Soon the shooting stopped. BJ held his position until he saw the cavalry detail reappear on the road. They were heading back in the opposite direction from which they had originally appeared, but at a much slower pace.

BJ climbed down out of the rocky fortress and mounted his horse. He rode out to meet up with the cavalry patrol and express his gratitude. When the leader of the patrol saw Sackett approaching them he held up his hand for the patrol to halt as he shouted out an order to a couple of his troopers.

"Johnson, you and Smith check out those three Indians and see if they're dead," the lieutenant called out. He then waited for Sackett.

"Am I glad you boys happened along," BJ said as he rode up to the patrol.

"We had gotten several reports of some Kiowa activity along the road here and were out trying to find the raiding party. They hit a couple of small ranches just north of here last week. How long were they in pursuit of you," the lieutenant asked?

"Not long; this big hearted animal almost ran their horses into the ground," BJ said as he patted the horse's neck.

"You're lucky. There were two men who didn't fare so well last week. To be honest, I'm surprised the war party was still in this area. I'm sure they figured we'd start patrolling this stretch of road," the lieutenant said with a perplexed look on his face.

"Yeah, that's not like the Kiowa I ever heard of. Usually they'll hit and run; never staying too long in one place. A lot like the Apache," BJ agreed.

Just then one of the other cavalry men called out, "Hey, Lieutenant...they're all three dead, Sir; but they ain't Indians."

The lieutenant frowned deeply as he answered, "What do you mean they're not Indians?"

"Just that, Sir; these men are white men made up to look like Kiowa," the trooper replied.

"Well I'll be..." the lieutenant said as both he and Sackett reined their horses in the direction of the three dead men.

"Why would white men dress up like Kiowa and attack strangers...unless it was simply to rob them," Sackett pondered.

"That's what I would guess their motive was; robbery. They do the robbing and killing if need be and the Kiowa get blamed for it," the lieutenant said with a scowl on his young face.

"Maybe they're the same ones who attacked the ranches you were telling me about," BJ said thoughtfully.

"That very well could be. We had some Kiowa escape from the stockade at the fort, that's why we figured it to be Indians in the first place. Maybe we were a little hasty in our judgment."

"Well, I'd better get a move on. I'd like to get on into town and get a good meal and sleep. After this little scrape I'll need it," BJ said as he prepared to move on.

"Good luck, friend," the lieutenant said and extended his gloved hand.

"Thank you, Lieutenant; right back at you," BJ said with a smile as he shook the officer's hand.

As Sackett rode away he looked back and saw the patrol rounding up the dead men's horses so they could take them back to the fort. He couldn't help but wonder about all this. He'd heard of incidents like this before, but not very often. He shook his head at the thought of how devious the human mind could be.

His next stop was not that far away, now. He'd spend the night in Fredericksburg and head out early the next day. Now all he wanted to do was eat something and get some much needed rest. He smiled when he had the thought that he was getting too old for this.

8

The Sheriff of Laredo stood in the doorway of the small bar and looked around the room. In the far left hand corner he saw who it was he was looking for; Brent Sackett, although he didn't know his name.

Pushing the swinging doors aside the sheriff entered and walked up to the bar, giving Sackett a long glance. Brent watched the sheriff from under the brim of his hat without moving his head, as the lawman moved across the room.

The sheriff gave Sackett one last glance as he walked up to the bar, "Say, Dan, give me a beer. How long has that fella in the corner been sitting over there, anyway?"

The barkeep looked in the direction the sheriff indicated, "Not long...maybe forty five minutes, but no more than that."

"Did you ever see him before?"

"Nope, can't say as I have. Well, not since yesterday when he came in for the first time. Why, is he wanted for something?"

"I don't know. There's just something about him that is familiar. Has anyone talked to him; you know, like they know him?"

"No, he's been alone except for Molly. She waited on him a couple of times and seemed to be smitten by him, the way she laughed at whatever it was he said to her," the bartender said.

"Do me a favor, would you? Let me know if he meets up with anyone here in the bar. I have a feeling about that guy that just won't go away," the sheriff said as he took a long draw from his beer glass.

Just then someone else entered the barroom. Every head in the place turned and looked at the two men who had entered; mainly because of the fanfare they entered with.

The lead man bellowed out "Ladies and gentlemen, you are all invited to attend the Royal Players stage production of Shakespeare's Hamlet. The show will begin at 7 p.m. this evening in the Silver Slipper Saloon, just down the street."

"Hey," the bartender called out with a frown plastered across his face, "Don't come in here and advertise something taking place at one of my competitors'."

"My dear fellow, you have no competitors where the great Shakespeare is involved. This is culture, not commercialism," the fancy dressed actor replied.

"Oh, are you doing the show for nothing," the bartender replied?

"An actor is worthy of his hire," the actor responded.

"So commercialism is involved here. Well what I said still stands then. Don't try and lure my customers away with your advertising; not in my establishment, anyway."

"How rude and uncouth," the actor said with a toss of his head. "Come, Jarvis, let us go to a more accommodating place of business."

With that the two men exited with the same embellished actions with which they had entered. The patrons all looked at one another and then went back to whatever they were doing before the extravagant entrance by the actor and his attendant.

"What the devil was that," the sheriff asked with a perplexed look on his face?

"Every time that troupe comes through here he does that. He knows the minute he walks in here that I don't want him doing it, but he does it anyway," Dan, the bartender said.

"Have you ever seen their show," the sheriff asked?

"No, and I don't plan on it. I can't understand half of what Shakespeare wrote so why would I want to go and sit through one of his plays."

"I see what you mean, Dan," the sheriff said as he downed the remainder of his beer.

After wiping his mouth with the back of his shirtsleeve the sheriff said, "Remember what I said about that hombre over there in the corner, Dan. I'll check back after awhile."

"Will do," Dan said as the sheriff turned and headed for the door.

Brent Sackett watched the sheriff exit and then glanced back in the direction of the bartender. From past experience he knew pretty much what the sheriff had told the bartender to do. He'd play a little mind game with the two of them. Why not have a little fun out of this whole thing.

When he finished the drink in front of him he got up as though he were about to leave. Just then two men entered who would work perfectly for his little ruse. He waited until the two hard looking men had taken a seat, also away from the bar, and walked over to them.

In a quiet voice so the bartender could not hear he began his conversation with the two.

"Say, aren't you boys from the Dallas area?"

The two men looked hard at Sackett; neither answering right away. Finally the one with a five day growth of beard replied.

"We ain't from that part of the country. Who are you anyway?"

"I used to be sheriff up there. I had a feeling we'd met, that's all. I wanted to pass along a word of warning. The sheriff was in here earlier asking everyone if they had seen two men that pretty much match your description. It was something about a payroll robbery. Are you from around here?"

The two men gave each other a quick glance before the one with the lesser growth of beard answered.

"We're just passing through on our way north. We've been doing some prospecting down in Mexico. Did that sheriff have any names to go with those descriptions," the man asked?

"Nope, just that they were about your size and weight. I wouldn't worry too much about it though; not since you're coming from Mexico," Sackett grinned, and then added, "Well, I just thought I knew you. You boys take care. I'll see you around," he said and looked in the direction of the bartender.

"Oh, yeah; the sheriff told the bartender to keep a sharp eye out for anyone answering that description, so he might be sending someone to fetch the sheriff. Like I said, just a head's up," Sackett said hoping to get the proper response from the two.

'Thanks for that," the heavy bearded man said.

"Adios," Sackett said and slowly walked out of the saloon.

Once outside he laughed to himself. The bartender would tell the sheriff about this meeting and the sheriff would start trying to keep them all three under surveillance. Now, however, the sheriff's concern would be more on the other two than on him. To the sheriff's way of thinking this was now a gang, not just one stranger in town.

Sackett headed off to the back streets of Laredo; to what the locals called the 'red light' district. The term 'red light' had been coined from the homes of prostitutes who had opened up shop along the railroad lines. When they were open for business they would hang a red lantern out to advertise it. He could use some feminine companionship. He'd head across the Rio Grande the next day; leaving the sheriff to wonder where he'd gone, while keeping busy watching the two men he'd just met in the bar.

He walked along the narrow street and looked at each woman who stood or sat outside the long row of attached adobe built homes. Each woman had a look or a comment for the tall, good looking Gringo. He would give each a quick glance and then look away. Finally he saw the one he would spend the night with; she was very pretty.

As he approached her she got up from the chair in which she had lounged and smiled warmly. The two didn't speak; she simply took his hand and led him inside the two room house. Entering the bedroom, Sackett latched the door as a safety measure. He'd heard too many stories of the way some of the Mexican women operated.

The woman couldn't have been over twenty one years of age, but was already getting what Sackett considered hardness to her big dark brown eyes. He tossed a twenty dollar gold piece onto a small table that stood by the bed.

The woman's eyes widened when she saw the money and then she smiled, showing very even, very white teeth.

Sackett removed his gun belt and sat down on the bed where he started to pull off his boots. Before he knew it the young woman grabbed his right boot and turned her backside towards him. He put his foot on her firm bottom and gave a push. The boot came off but not what you would call easily. The same thing was done for the left foot, only this time Brent's push sent her all the way to the door. Turning around and facing him, she leaned back against the door. He gave her an approving smile, which she returned with a seductive grin. Brent didn't see her unlatch the door as she moved away from it.

The young woman stood in front of him and slowly began to pull her cream colored peasant blouse up over her head. She tossed the blouse on a chair next to the bed; she wore no undergarments and stood before him naked from the waist up. Her breasts and midriff were a shade lighter than the light cocoa coloring of her face, shoulders, and arms.

Brent grinned and again nodded his approval. She slowly began to slip out of her long skirt which matched the blouse in color. She was a vision of beauty as she stood there totally naked before him.

He held out his hand and she moved towards him. When she took his hand he stood up and faced her. He slipped his arm around her tiny waist and pulled her up close to him. Looking down into her ebony eyes he tenderly kissed her full and eager lips.

Suddenly and violently the door to the bedroom burst open and two men rushed in. Before Sackett could react one of the men hit him across the head with a large wooden club, knocking him to his knees. While he was down the other man attempted to kick him in the head, but Sackett managed to move just enough to catch a glancing blow.

The woman moved quickly out of the way and watched as the two men attempted to overpower her would-be lover. The blow to the head had addled Sackett, but he had not lost consciousness. An adrenalin rush cleared his head quickly and he sprang to his feet.

He hit the man wielding the club in the face with a hard right hand, causing the man to step back two full steps. He spun quickly around and hit the smaller of the two men a hard shot in the ribs which caved the man to one side. Grabbing the man with the club by the arm he slung the man into the shorter of the two, sending them both sprawling across the bed.

Sackett grabbed his gun belt and pulled his pistol from its holster. He fired two quick shots, both of them finding their mark. The two men fell back on the bed; one was critically wounded and the other was stone cold dead. Sackett looked at the woman who stood there holding a knife towards him; a knife she had picked up off the table after the two men had entered.

The look on her face went from anger to fear when she saw that Sackett had the pistol pointed at her and then heard the deadly sound made as he cocked the hammer back. His frown was deep as he glared at the woman who had attempted to set him up.

"That was a very bad mistake, senorita; adios," he said.

He fired one shot that struck the young woman in the breast bone, knocking her back onto the bed with the two other conspirators. Sackett walked over to the bed and moved the woman's feet to one side as he sat down and slipped his boots back on.

He stood up and strapped his gun belt on and then looked at the three people he'd just shot. A look of disgust expressed his feelings about the entire incident. He shook his head as he put his hat on and headed out the door.

"Amateurs," he said quietly, "rank amateurs."

He walked out of the house and on down the street. He didn't see anyone watching him, but there were at least six sets of eyes watching the tall man walk away from the house that contained the three bodies.

The Laredo sheriff looked anxiously at the doctor when he emerged from the room where he had just operated on two of the shooting victims.

"When can I talk to one of them, Doc," the sheriff asked?

"I don't know that you will, Sheriff. Both of them are in pretty bad shape. If you want to know who shot them I'd start talking to some of the neighbors. I'm not sure I can pull either of these two through."

"The neighbors don't want to tell me anything. They'd just as soon let the guilty go free as help the law in any way. No, my only hope is that one of these two will pull through long enough for me to get some answers. I'm not even sure they'll talk to me, though. Craziest bunch of people I've ever seen," the sheriff mused.

"It doesn't surprise me that bad luck finally caught up with Ramona. I'd say this is the work of someone she and her brothers tried to hustle, not taking it. Those three have been accused of more shenanigans than the James boys, the Younger brothers, and the Daltons combined."

"I know, but I can't have shooting like this taking place down here; not if I want to keep my job," the sheriff said and then grew quiet.

"What is it; why so quiet all of a sudden?"

"I was just thinking about a new face in town. I wonder where he was when all this shooting was taking place," the sheriff wondered aloud.

"New face...he must not have sat in on any of the poker games I was involved in or I would remember him; all the men sitting in on those games had the same, tired old faces I've looked at for...well, too many years," the doctor laughed.

"Say Doc, if you should happen to hear any rumors around about the one responsible for shooting these three, would you please let me know. Like I said, if I want to keep my job I've got to drop the hammer on someone for this."

"Yeah, sure; if I hear anything," the doctor replied.

9

Earl Rule glared hard at the picture from the newspaper article that he held in his hands. He finally looked up at the man sitting across the table from him.

"And you're positive that this here is the man who shot Johnny down in cold blood, is that right," Earl said viciously?

"I'm sure, Earl. I remember him because I entered the saloon just behind him. This article with his picture was in the Crystal City Sentinel last year. I remembered it after I got back to the office and found this article in my desk. I was in Crystal City at the time of the attempted bank robbery and brought this copy of the newspaper home with me.

"It's just like the article says, he stopped an attempted holdup of the bank there. His name is Brent Sackett; he was a deputy sheriff back then; maybe he still is," Grover Dugan, the editor of the Coleman Crier, a weekly newspaper stated.

"I'll take that over to the saloon and see if the sheriff can remember what the man looked like," Earl said as he turned to go.

"Be sure and bring that paper back. I use it for a model for the Crier," Dugan called after Rule.

Rupert and Cory were all ready in the saloon owned by the sheriff. One of the girls who worked the saloon was standing next to Cory's chair with her hand on his shoulder while he played out a poker hand. When Earl walked in and saw his two sons playing cards he uttered a swear word under his breath and headed towards the poker table.

Walking up behind Cory and the young woman, Earl grabbed her by the arm and yanked her back. Cory spun around at the sudden intrusion with a scowl on his face. The angry glare dropped instantly when he saw that the intruder was his pa.

"I didn't send you two no goods in here to play cards, damn your hide. I told you to ask around about Johnny's killer," Earl said, spitting the words out.

"We did, Pa, we did," Cory said as he threw his hands up to protect his face from the blow he expected, but didn't receive.

"You pick up your money and let's go. I'm going to talk to that worthless sheriff over there and then we're going looking for a man named Brent Sackett," Earl growled.

"Who's Brent Sackett," Rupert asked?

"That's the man's name that killed Johnny. Now come on," Earl ordered.

The boys started to pick up their money off the table when one of the men, a stranger in Coleman, objected.

"You boys have some of my money and I'd like to have a chance to win it back," the man said.

Earl turned towards the man with a look of shear hatred.

"You shouldn't have lost it in the first place, stranger," Earl snarled.

"And you shouldn't talk to me the way you're doing," the stranger replied evenly.

"What; do you know who you're talking to," Earl snapped?

"I don't know and I don't care," the stranger said as he slowly stood up.

"Do you have a name; so they'll know what to put on your tombstone when they bury you," Earl said as he took a gunman's stance.

"Yes I do. My friends call me Wes. On my tombstone, when the time comes, they'll put John Wesley Hardin," the stranger said slowly.

"Pa, that's Wes Hardin. He's killed men for just looking at him wrong," Cory said wide eyed.

Earl's anger quickly subsided. He'd never faced a man with a real reputation as being a gunfighter. Now it was different. From what he'd heard, Hardin enjoyed showdowns like this.

"Anyone could say they're John Wesley Hardin," Earl said his words taking on a much softer tone.

"I guess they could at that. If they were trying to say they were me, though, they'd be lying. Now if you want to go for your gun...and that includes you boys there...go ahead. I'll kill all three of you," Hardin said with true confidence.

Earl looked quickly around the room. He didn't like losing face, but it was better than losing his life as well as his boy's. He slowly moved his hand away from his pistol and backed up while turning around.

When he spotted the sheriff he saw his way out.

"Sheriff, I came in here to talk to you about the man who gunned down Johnny."

He walked towards the sheriff with Hardin watching him for a few seconds before setting down. Hardin looked at Cory and Rupert and grinned.

"Now, boys, have a seat and let's play some poker."

Earl pulled the paper clipping out of his shirt and handed it to the sheriff. The sheriff took it and looked at the picture with accompanying story.

"What's this, Earl," the sheriff asked?

"Take a look at the man in the picture. Is this the man who killed Johnny?"

The sheriff studied the picture and his countenance suddenly brightened, "Why, yes, by Jove that is the man."

"His name is Brent Sackett. I want you to remember that name and if he comes back through here you arrest him, do you hear me," Earl demanded.

"I can hold him for a time, but not for long," the sheriff stated.

"Just time enough to notify me and my boys," Earl said with a frown.

"Your boys...you mean the ones who are back in the poker game over there?"

Earl looked towards the poker table and then back at the sheriff, "That's the ones; the ones playing cards with John Wesley Hardin. Isn't he wanted for something in Texas?"

"Not that I know of," the sheriff responded quickly.

"You wouldn't admit it even if you knew it to be true," Earl said with contempt.

"Well, I guess I could always call on you to arrest him; if he was wanted for something that is," the sheriff said slowly, turning the slur on Rule.

"You'll get yours someday; of that I am sure."

"Won't we all," the sheriff said, getting in the last word.

BJ Sackett stepped down off his mount at the Forbes Livery Stable in San Antonio. The owner came out of his small office and greeted his new customer.

"Howdy, what can I do for you," the man asked?

"I'd like to put my horse up for the night; feed, water, and curry," BJ said.

"That'll be fifty cents," the man replied.

BJ tossed him a silver dollar and told him to keep it in case he decided to stay another day. The man grinned as he nodded yes.

"You wouldn't happen to know a man around here by the name of Myron Selman, would you," he asked?

The man frowned slightly as he mulled over the name, "No, I can't say as I have. Has he lived down here long?"

"Not for awhile; he's been punching cattle up north around Abilene. He came back down here to get back with a gal he knew here," BJ explained.

"You don't happen to know her name do you?"

"No, I sure don't. It's him I'm interested in and he never told me her name."

"Myron Selman...actually the name of Selman does sound familiar, but not Myron. I'm sorry I can't be of more help," the man said.

"Thanks anyway. I was just taking a shot in the dark. I'll ask around at some of the local saloons; there's, probably, where I'll have more luck," BJ smiled.

"If you need a room I suggest you try Amanda's Boarding House and it's just down the street there. She has the best and most reasonable place in town. At least you won't get your valuables or boots stolen while you sleep," the man laughed.

"Amanda's; thanks I'll check it out," BJ said with a wave as he turned and headed out the door for his short walk into town.

Amanda's Boarding House was the first two story structure that BJ came to. He carried his bedroll under his left arm and his Winchester in his right hand. As he opened the door a bell over the threshold announced his entrance.

Sackett looked around the neatly decorated room and smiled at the homey atmosphere. Just then a young woman rounded the corner and smiled warmly.

"Hello, may I help you," she asked?

BJ's eyes brightened at the sight of the pretty young lady. He stumbled over his words, but managed to answer.

"Yes'm, uh ma'am; I'd like a bed...I mean a room."

She stifled a smile as she answered, "How long would you like a bed," she teased, but in a serious tone of voice.

"The longest you've got, I guess. As you can see I'm well over six feet tall," BJ replied, recognizing her teasing remark.

She could no longer hold back the laugh, which was as lilting as a gentle babbling brook.

"Actually, I don't know how long I'll need a ... room. It may be for a couple of nights, but could be longer," Sackett said more seriously, but still with a smile.

"My name is Amanda Hefner, but my friends all call me Mandy; I'm the owner of the boarding house. What name should I put in the register?"

"BJ, uh Brian Sackett," BJ said as he shifted his rifle to his left hand.

He set his bedroll on the floor and signed the register. Mandy causally looked at the name he'd penned and then commented.

"Brian Sackett, just like you said," she grinned.

"Yep, it hasn't changed since I was born."

She smiled as she picked a key off a hook behind the counter.

"If you'll follow me I'll show you where you're room is," she said as she walked towards the stairs.

She led him upstairs to the room directly in front of the staircase. She unlocked the door and then handed the key to BJ. He took the key and looked into her eyes. She had very kind eyes, but with a mischievous glint to them.

"If there's anything you need, please call on me. You'll find water in the basin should you want to freshen up. We have a bathroom at the end of the hall," she said and pointed to it.

"A bathroom...indoors," BJ said with a slight frown?

"One of the wonders of advances in modern engineering," Mandy replied.

"A bathroom indoors; what will they think of next," BJ said with a shake of his head.

"We have breakfast at six o'clock sharp; lunch at twelve noon; and dinner at six o'clock sharp. We have a wonderful cook who prides herself in serving a good meal," Mandy stated.

"Oh, is that right. I'll have to make it a point to show my appreciation then. It looks like I only have to wait about three hours and I can have dinner."

"I'll see you there," Mandy said as she started to go back down the stairs.

"I'll be looking forward to it," BJ said as he opened wide the door to his room. As an afterthought he added, "Oh, could you tell me where the best saloon in town is?"

He then realized how the question had sounded and quickly began to try and cover up his faux pas.

"Not that you would know that; I mean, go there...to the best saloon in town, that is...not that you would go to a bad saloon...I mean, you could if you wanted to...uh...aw shucks, do you?"

Mandy began to laugh which quickly eased BJ's embarrassment. He shook his head and said, "I don't know what it is about you, but suddenly I can't get my words straight."

"I think it's charming," Mandy chuckled as she eyed the tall, good looking man who was now one of her boarders. "As a matter of fact, I do know the whereabouts of the best saloon in San Antonio. Not that I go there, mind you; but, if you head your nose on down the street and just follow it, you'll see the saloon on your right about three blocks from here."

"Thank you, ma'am; I'm not going there to drink, just so you know," BJ said seriously.

"Oh, and what are you going there for, if you don't mind my asking," Mandy asked slightly raising one eyebrow?

Realizing his remark could be taken the wrong way, again, he quickly backtracked.

"Oh, no not that...uh, you know. Actually I'm looking for someone. A man...I mean I'm trailing a man."

Mandy cocked her head to one side, "Oh, are you a lawman?"

"No, I'm not, but the man I'm tracking is an outlaw. He's wanted for shooting my brother up near Abilene."

"Abilene, Kansas or Texas," Mandy asked?

"Texas, ma'am, Abilene, Texas," BJ answered.

"I see; does this man that you're following have a name?"

"Yes, ma'am, he sure does. It's Myron Selman."

Mandy's eyes narrowed. She raised her head slightly and then once again cocked it to one side.

"Myron Selman," she inquired curiously?

"That's right...do you know him?"

"You might say that; he's my sister's fiancé."

Now it was Brian's turn to look puzzled. What a coincidence this was turning out to be; now to find out where Selman was at that time.

"Is he here?"

"Yes, he's here, but I'd like to know more about this shooting you say he was involved in before I tell you where he's at."

"Ma'am, I didn't come to kill him, not unless he wants to make a fight of it. I just want to take him back to stand trial," Brian said honestly.

"Wait here, please," Mandy said and went down the hall.

Brian slowly unbuckled his gun belt and set it inside his room on a chair. He reached behind his back and touched the grip of the pistol he carried tucked in his belt; a habit he'd gotten into during the War.

He watched as Mandy rapped lightly on a door, two doors down from his, and then stepped back. Myron Selman opened the door and when he saw Mandy grinned and stepped out into the hallway.

"Myron, there's someone here who'd like to speak with you," Mandy said evenly.

"Oh, sure, who is it," Myron said and looked down the hallway.

When he saw BJ standing there a look of surprise came to his face, but quickly faded. He didn't try to run or anything even close to it; instead he walked down the hallway towards BJ.

"Say BJ, what brings you down here?"

"You do, Myron. I came to take you back to stand trial," BJ said stone faced.

"Stand trial; what are you talking about? Stand trial for what?"

"Don't play dumb with me, Myron. You know damned good and well what for; for shooting AJ...he may be dead now, for all I know," BJ said tight lipped.

"What do you mean, for shooting AJ? Why would I do a thing like that? Hey, I was sore for the firing, but I sure wouldn't do something as stupid...or as lowdown, as that."

"Then you don't have a thing to worry about, do you?"

"I'm not making that long ride back to Abilene to stand trial for something I know nothing about," Selman stated firmly.

"Oh, I think you will; that's why I'm here," BJ came back.

"When did this shooting take place, anyway?"

"The afternoon I let you go. I figure you were sore over the firing and came back for your revenge, except it was AJ who answered the door."

"After I packed up my belongings I lit out for here. There was nothing holding me up there, not then; that's for sure. In fact I was glad to leave. I cut off the main road to knock about five miles off, so I didn't see anyone until I'd gone a good ten miles or so. Who was it said they saw me shoot AJ, any way?"

"Wes Baggett; he saw you riding away from the ranch house after AJ was shot."

"Wes Baggett; then he's lying through his teeth. Wes Baggett, now there's a fine one to be taking his word on for anything. Why, he'd lie about his own mother if it would put a dollar in his pocket."

"Wes is our top hand; a good cowboy and a good friend."

"He's not the friend you might think he is, BJ."

"What do you mean by that?"

"You know he's taken up with Logan Miller, right?"

"Right, so," BJ replied curiously?

"And you know that Logan Miller has a prison record, right?"

"Yeah, for a crime he didn't commit; or so he claims."

"Oh he committed a crime all right and one that he could, and would have been hanged for, if a US Marshal hadn't arrived just before the hanging took place. He was involved in stealing cattle from a rancher that he was working for at the time. It was in the Lubbock area. I think it was a little settlement called Sundown.

"I'd bet my last dollar that the cattle you were missing that we thought might be getting off into that 'black water' mess on the ranch, are in fact in a pen somewhere waiting to have the brand changed."

"That's a mighty strong accusation, Myron. Where'd you get your information about this? Who'd you hear this from, anyway?"

"That guy that came to the ranch looking for work just before we left on that last drive; I think he said his name was Ray Clayton or Clanton...something like that anyway. He recognized Miller while we were talking and he told me about it. He'd worked for the same rancher. Whatever happened to that guy, anyway? I thought you gave him a job?"

"I gave him a job, but he never came back to the ranch. He said he had to go back into town to get his belongings. That's the last we saw of him," BJ said thoughtfully. "I don't suppose you have any proof to back it up, do you; other than that guy's words?"

"No, but I'll bet I could find some proof if given half a chance. Contacting the rancher in Sundown would be a good place to start."

"I'll give you that chance by taking you back to Abilene with me and telling your story in a court of law," Sackett said firmly.

"I'm not going to make that ride again; not when I've got a job to go on down here in San Antonio."

"I'll take you back one way or another; either in the saddle or across it. The choice is yours," Sackett said with a steady gaze.

"How; you ain't even wearing a gun. Now, if I had gunned down AJ do you think I would have stood here and talked to you as long as we have? No, I'd have shot it out with you right here," Myron said evenly.

Mandy had been taking all this in and not saying a word; her eyes shifting from one man to the next, as they spoke. Now it was her turn to speak.

"I'll not have any shooting in my place. If you have a dispute you take it to the local authorities and straighten it out. As long as you two are under this roof I am the boss and you'll do as you're told," she said firmly.

The two men looked at her and then back at one another. Selman shook his head slightly as he answered her.

"Mandy, I ain't planning on doing nothing of a violent nature in here or anywhere else. I had my fill of killing when I had to kill that man while on my last cattle drive. It's not something I want to do again."

Sackett looked at Selman warily, and then at the young woman, and then back at Selman.

"I'm not leaving this town without you, Selman. But I'm willing to make this place a sanctuary of sorts. The first time you try anything though, this sanctuary will become your burial ground, do you hear me?"

"I'm not going to try anything, Sackett. You said there was a lawman looking for me and that was the reason you let me go. You didn't give me a chance to explain that the lawman is related to the man I killed. He didn't come to arrest me, he came to kill me. I didn't tell you at the time, but I was going to quit when I heard that he was in Abilene."

"Why didn't you tell me all this the day I fired you," BJ questioned?

"I didn't think it would matter none. Besides, I had to get out of there, so what was the point. BJ, if you'll listen to what I have to say, I think you're going to understand the shooting of your brother a lot better; the shooting I had nothing to do with."

"You tell a great story Selman. If only half of what you say is true it would change the entire picture I've formed of you, but I'm still not convinced you're telling me the truth. I've heard too many contradictions in the stories involving you. Right now I don't know what to believe."

"I've leveled with you. Ask Mandy if I've ever been in any trouble that she knows about. She knows me as well as anyone. I've been engaged to her sister for over a year; that was another reason I went north looking for work."

"He's never been in any kind of trouble around here, Mr. Sackett; if he had I'd have heard about it. In fact, I don't think he's capable of anything criminal. I'll swear that on a stack of Bibles," Mandy said sincerely.

A lot of what Selman had said got BJ to thinking. He'd never questioned what Wes Baggett told him. Maybe he should have? They had been missing a lot of cattle at the ranch; cattle they'd left behind from their last drive to use in building another herd. Maybe, just maybe, Selman was telling the truth. Only time would tell for sure.

"We'll talk about this later. Until then, don't get any crazy notions about skipping out of here. I found you once and I'll find you again, no matter where you go. One other thing; if you should run I'll know you're guilty," BJ said through slightly clenched teeth.

10

BJ Sackett sat and stared across the dining room table at Selman who tried not to notice. Was he telling the truth or not? After their initial conversation BJ had recalled a number of things he'd put out of his mind until now.

For one thing Wes Baggett and Logan Miller had seemed to hit it off from the first day Miller hired on. BJ remembered his pa had mentioned that the two almost seemed to know one another. Now he began to think maybe they had.

Also, while on the last cattle drive to the railhead, he recalled the local sheriff of one of the towns along the trail had came out to the herd looking for two men he said had robbed a small store in town. Wes and Miller didn't come in with the others, so he had not been able to take a look at them. When asked about it, they said they were keeping an eye on a band of Indians in the area to make sure they didn't try to steal any of the herd. Now he wondered.

"Would you care for another glass of wine, Mr. Sackett," Mandy asked as she held the decanter out?

"I don't mind if I do. That's a very good wine," BJ replied.

"She stomps the grapes with her own two feet," Myron said with a grin.

"Oh, stop it," Mandy laughed.

"On second thought, maybe I'd better pass on the wine," BJ said, surprised that he would even share in a joke with Selman. "That dinner was very good, by the way. You are right about your cook. She is good."

Mandy blushed slightly at the compliment, dropping her eyes and then casting a quick glance in Selman's direction.

"So what is it you do, Mr. Sackett," one of the other guests staying in the boarding house asked? "Oh, my name is Brownlee, by the way;...Cyril Brownlee."

"Nice to make your acquaintance, Mr. Brownlee," BJ answered, "I'm a rancher. My father...brother and I," he said and cast a quick glance at Selman, "have a ten thousand acre spread near Abilene."

"Ten thousand acres, huh; that's a good sized ranch," the man answered.

"There are a lot bigger ones. We're happy though. What do you do?"

"I'm a doctor of medicine. Mainly though I am into maintenance of one's well being. I have dedicated my life to discovering how to strengthen one's immune system. I believe defense is the best medicine. If you have a strong immune system you are less likely to fall prey to many of the various diseases out there that attack the human body," the man said going into a well practiced oratory.

"Dr Brownlee is a traveling medicine man. He has his wagon right out back," Mandy said with a knowing smile.

"Yes, the young lady is right. I travel far and wide spreading the good news of my invention and medicinal concoction. Perhaps you would like to try a bottle," the doctor asked?

"Maybe later; but right now I'm going to try some of that wonderful blackberry cobbler I heard we were going to have for dessert," BJ replied. "If it's anything like the dinner we're in for a treat. Not only is the lady pretty, but she's a great cook to boot."

"She's going to make some lucky fella a wonderful wife," Selman said and then took on a look that indicated he'd spoken out of turn. BJ hadn't caught that, however.

"I was just wondering about that. I'm surprised you're not married; a beautiful, young woman, like yourself," BJ remarked.

Mandy's countenance changed severely as she looked down at the napkin folded in her lap. Sackett knew he had touched a sore spot; but, Selman had started the subject; he was just commenting.

"I'm sorry, Mandy...I shouldn't have said what I did," Selman said as he looked at his future sister-in-law sorrowfully.

Mandy looked quickly at the dinner guests with a weak smile and then stood up, "Please excuse me. I have some work to do in the kitchen."

With that she picked up her plate and silverware and walked towards the kitchen.

Everyone at the table watched her departure, but no one said anything until Mandy's sister, Gina Hefner entered the conversation.

"Maybe I should explain...Mandy was engaged until six months ago, but her fiancé was killed in an argument over a land deal. We have a man here in San Antonio who is trying to buy the entire town, or so it seems. He is forcing some of the business owners to sell by buying their mortgages and then raising the payment rate so they can't afford it. Mandy's fiancé confronted him, an argument ensued and he was gunned down by one of the man's hired killers."

"You shouldn't have touched on that subject, Myron," Gina said.

"I know; I just didn't think," Selman answered.

"I didn't help matters either," BJ offered.

"You had no way of knowing. She'll be all right; just give her a few minutes to collect herself."

BJ downed the rest of his wine and started to get up. Suddenly the room seemed to tilt slightly causing him to sit back down and close his eyes. He looked around the room at the four other people at the table and shook his head.

"Are you all right, Mr. Sackett," Gina queried?

"Yeah, just a little dizzy, that's all. I must be more tired than I realized," BJ said and closed his eyes again to try and shake the dizzy spell.

Things cleared momentarily and he tried to stand up once again. Once on his feet the room began to spin and everything began to swim before him. The next thing he knew he was falling, and that was the last thing he remembered until he awoke the next morning.

When BJ opened his eyes he found himself staring up into the face of a kindly looking gentleman. It was the doctor who was staying in the boarding house; the traveling medicine man.

"Well, welcome back to the land of the living," the doctor said with a smile.

"Wha ... what happened," BJ asked?

"You had a little too much to drink after being so tired from your long journey, I'd say."

BJ closed his eyes and shook his head to clear his vision which slowly returned to normal.

"Since when is two glasses of wine too much," he said; his mouth dry as if he'd swallowed a bole of cotton.

"I think what you need is some of my magic elixir; it will pick you right up," the doctor said as he poured a spoonful of the sweet tasting, syrupy concoction from its bottle.

"Open wide," he said as he pinched BJ nose to get him to open his mouth.

BJ was prepared for the worst, but the elixir tasted like a mix between honey and maple syrup with a pinch of rum thrown in. That's what ninety-nine percent of the elixir was, in fact.

"There my boy, you'll feel better in no time," the doctor said.

The sound of a bird chirping outside BJ's bedroom window caused him to sit upright in bed. The doctor moved back with eyes wide and smiled.

"My, my, it looks like my tonic is working faster than I thought it would," the doctor said excitedly.

"What time is it," BJ questioned?

"Oh...it's a little past ten o'clock," the doc said as he looked at his pocket watch.

"Where's Selman," was BJ next question?

"Selman...oh, he was up and around early this morning. In fact, I saw him ride off around six o'clock this morning," the doctor said scratching his head.

BJ jumped out of bed, but had to sit back down and close his eyes for a moment still fighting a little of the dizziness he'd suffered the night before. Just then the door to his room opened slightly and Mandy looked in.

"Oh, I see you're awake," she asked with a weak smile.

"What did you put in that wine you gave me," BJ snapped angrily?

"Why, nothing...you saw me pour wine in the other's glasses from the same decanter I poured yours. Perhaps it's like the doctor said and it was a combination of being tired from your journey," she said trying to defend herself.

"No, that's not what it was; you put something in the wine or the food, something. Where did Selman go?"

"I can't tell you that," Mandy said tersely.

"You mean you won't tell me, don't you," BJ said as he once again tried to stand, this time making it.

When he realized he was standing there in just his long johns, he quickly grabbed the blanket off the bed and wrapped it around him.

"Where's my pants," he demanded?

"How would I know? I certainly didn't undress you," Mandy replied haughtily.

"Would somebody please get me my pants," BJ said raising his voice at least two levels.

"Oh, I think these are what you're looking for young man," the doctor said as he looked down on the floor on the opposite side of the bed from where Sackett was standing.

BJ rushed around the bed and grabbed his pants from the doctor and quickly slipped them on. He looked around for his boots, but didn't see them right away.

"My boots," he yelled!

"They're over there," Mandy said and pointed towards the window.

Sackett rushed to the window only to find one boot, but not the other. Grabbing it up he looked around quickly and spotted the other boot on the opposite side of the room from the one he'd picked up by the window.

The same desperate question followed concerning the whereabouts of his gun and holster which was behind a chair next to the window. His shirt was hanging on a hook behind the door.

Once fully dressed he grabbed his rifle and bedroll and headed towards the door. When he drew near to Mandy he glared at her.

"Where's Selman?"

"How should I know, I'm not engaged to him," Mandy said evenly.

"Arghh..." BJ growled and rushed out of the room.

He figured that Selman had decided to make a run for it and they had drugged him to give him a head start. Why had he waited until six o'clock in the morning though? Then BJ remembered that Selman had said something about having found a job down there in San Antonio. Maybe he had acted too hastily in assuming that Selman had made a run for it.

He stopped at the front door and turned to go back upstairs. Just as he did Mandy and the doctor came down the stairs.

"Where is this place that Selman went to work at?"

"Oh, it's the Lazy J about five miles out of town," Mandy said and then caught herself.

"In which direction," BJ snapped?

"I don't know that; I just know it's five miles out of town," she said coyly.

"Arghh...women," BJ said again as he turned and rushed out the door and headed for the livery stable.

When he reached the livery he asked the old man in the office how to get to the Lazy J ranch.

"Oh, you head out of town to the west about four or five miles and you'll come to a road that leads to the north. There used to be a sign there, but someone said the wind blew it down. We can get some wind down here at times," the old man said with a chuckle.

"So do I take the road to the north," BJ coaxed, trying desperately to hold his temper?

"Oh, yeah, you do. You'll go about a half mile and see the ranch house. It's a nice place; at least it used to be. I ain't been out there in a couple of years, but...," the old man droned on as BJ rushed to where his horse was stalled.

He saddled his horse quickly and mounted up. He figured he'd give Selman the benefit of the doubt and hope that he'd reported to work. Otherwise he'd really have no idea which direction the man headed; and he certainly was going to get no help from Mandy or her sister.

When BJ arrived at the Lazy J the first person he ran into was the ranch foreman. He inquired as to the new hire by the name of Myron Selman. The foreman shook his head slowly in a negative manner as he pondered the name.

"No, we ain't hired anyone recently by that name," he said and then looked towards the barn.

"He's the last man we hired and that was about two weeks ago," he said pointing towards a man who definitely was not Myron Selman.

"Thanks...it looks like I was sent on a wild goose chase by the lady that runs the boarding house in town," BJ said with a deep frown.

"You mean Mandy Hefner," the foreman asked?

"Yeah, that's right. Myron Selman is her sister's fiancé," BJ replied.

"Oh, is that his name. I knew she was engaged, but I didn't know the man's name. I don't know a lot of the people in town...too busy out here. I do know where he went to work though," the foreman offered.

"You do...where?"

"It's the Crooked T...it's about ten miles to the south. Just go back to the cross road and head south. You can't miss it; they have a big sign over the road to the ranch house."

"Thank you pardner," BJ said and headed back in the direction from which he'd come.

Meanwhile Myron Selman was headed for Laredo. He had a cousin who lived down there who would put him up until it was safe to return to San Antonio. He knew that Mandy, Gina, and the doctor would send him on a couple of false trails so there was no need to go back into town.

Selman was telling the truth about the lawman who had come to Abilene looking for him. He was related to the man he'd been forced to kill while on the cattle drive. In fact, Selman was telling the truth about everything he'd related to BJ, except where he had gotten a job. He sensed that Sackett was only going to believe what he wanted to believe, so the best thing for him was to take it on the run.

Selman headed south towards Crystal City. He knew a couple of people in that area who would put him up for a day or two and give him some supplies for the rest of the trip to Laredo. One of the people he knew there was the sheriff of Crystal City, Ben Cates.

It was a good three day ride from San Antonio to Crystal City, but fairly easy traveling. Selman felt bad about running out on Gina again. She'd been after him to get married and they thought his return to San Antonio would make it possible; especially after finding a job locally. Now this; and he's on the move again. Maybe this would be the last time he'd have to pull up stakes and head out. He certainly hoped so, anyway.

As he rode along he pulled the note she had written him from his shirt pocket. He read the short note again and smiled. The truth was that Selman had ulterior motives for marrying Gina. She would inherit a lot of money when she turned twenty four according to the will that the lawyer Gina had hired had told him; the lawyer who was also a friend of Selman. She was a beauty, but so was all that money she would be inheriting. He would never have to work as a cowhand again; unless, of course the cattle were his.

11

The doctor walked slowly into the kitchen at the Sackett ranch and sat down heavily. He looked at Loretta Sackett with a serious look on his face which caused her to expect the worst. Then a smile slowly made its way across the entire expanse of his tired face.

"You have one tough son in there, Loretta," the doctor began. "I can't believe the progress he's made over the past couple of days. It's nearing miracle stage, I'll tell you that much. I never thought he'd be this quick in recovering."

"Oh, Doctor, that is the best news I could possibly hear right now. So he's out of danger?"

"Out of danger; I'll say he's out of danger. Why at the rate he's recovering I'd say he'll be back at work in three, maybe four weeks. Of course, he'll have to take it easy at first, but I don't think he's going to have any side effects from this shooting," the doctor said as Loretta poured him a cup of freshly brewed coffee.

Just then the door opened and John Sackett walked in with a deep frown on his face. Loretta started to give him the good news about AJ, but waited to hear what was bothering John.

"Have you seen Wes lately," he asked?
"Not since breakfast, John, why," Loretta answered?
"I have a couple of questions for him. I just talked to Red Blankenship and he said he saw Wes and Logan Miller driving at least two dozen of our steers into a loading pen in Abilene. I didn't send him into town with any of our cattle, so I'd like to know whose cattle they were," John said tightly.
"Oh, I'm sure Wes has a good reason to be doing that," Loretta replied.
"We'll see. I don't want you to mention this to him or any one else. I'll put it to him after I give him a chance to come forward first with the information. I hope I'm wrong about this, but I think those two may be the cause of some of our losses lately," John said as he poured himself a cup of coffee.
"John, the doctor has really wonderful news about AJ. He said he's doing much better than expected and will probably be able to go back to work in a few weeks; isn't that right, Doctor," Loretta beamed?
"That's right. A near miracle," the doctor said repeating his previous statement.
"That is good news. I wish BJ was back here to hear the good news. We'll give thanks to the Lord this evening; properly that is."
"I already have," Loretta smiled.
John looked at the doctor, "You will stay for dinner, won't you Silas," he asked?
"No, I have another call to make and I'm going to have to get a move on if I'm going to get back to town before dark; but thanks for the offer. You know how I love Loretta's cooking," the doctor said with a wide grin.
"There'll be other times, I'm sure," John said with a nod.

Baggett counted out half the money he held in his calloused hands and handed it to Logan Miller as they walked out of the Wells Fargo Bank in Abilene. The two of them looked at one another and broke into a shared laugh.

"It beats punching cattle for a living, doesn't it Logan?"

"You said it, pardner," Logan responded.

"What do you say we go over and have a couple of beers before heading back to the ranch," Baggett said slapping his friend on the back.

The two of them went to the Abilene House and bellied up to the bar. They ordered two beers and once they had been served, started for a table in the back. As they walked past one of the two pool tables, Logan accidentally bumped a man preparing to make a shot. The jostling caused the man to miss badly. He spun around and glared at Miller.

"Why don't you watch where you're going, slew foot," the man snapped.

"What did you call me," Miller cracked back?

"Slew foot; like the old bear...you know clumsy and ugly," the man said with a snarl to his words.

"No one talks to me like that and gets away with it," Miller said turning and facing the man.

"I just did ... or didn't you hear me," the man said?

Miller threw the glass of beer he was holding into the man's face, followed with a hard right to the man's chin. The man's head snapped back, but he didn't go down. Miller followed the right hand with a left that sent a spray of blood shooting from the man's nose.

Baggett grinned at the ease with which his friend was handling the pool shooter. He gave out with a loud whoop as Miller moved in to finish the fight. His joy was short lived, however, when the man suddenly scrambled to his feet and grabbed one of the pool balls off the table, smashing it into the side of Miller's head.

The force of the blow sent Miller to one knee which allowed the man to hit him a chopping right hand, then a left, then another hard right. Miller fell to one side as the man leapt into the air and came down hard with both boots on Miller's face. The boots slid off, one on each side of Logan's face, leaving angry red marks.

The man wasn't finished, however. He kicked Miller in the ribs and drew his foot back to give him another hard shot when the bark of a pistol rang out. The man turned around slowly with a dazed look on his face. He put one hand to his side and when he removed his hand it was covered with blood. Wes Baggett had shot him.

The man stared glassy eyed at Baggett for a moment and then wavered slightly before crumpling to the floor. Baggett stood there with the smoking gun in his hand as the sheriff unexpectedly walked into the saloon.

"So...what were you and Logan doing in town, anyway," John Sackett asked his top hand through the bars of the town jail. "I hadn't sent you in here."

"Oh, uh, we had some business at the bank," Baggett said seriously; grabbing at the first excuse he thought of.

"Oh, what kind of business," John pressed?

"I owed Logan some money and he needed it so we rode in and I cashed a check I had in order to pay him off."

"I see. I heard you had a bill of sale for some cattle, Wes. Whose cattle did you sell, anyway," John continued?

"It wasn't yours Mr. Sackett. It was money I'd saved," Wes stammered.

"We're talking about the cattle here, Wes; not the money. Whose cattle did you sell...it wasn't Sackett cattle was it?"

"No, they were mavericks we'd rounded up. They didn't have a brand and Logan and I put our own brand on them, that's all," Wes said feeling he'd covered himself adequately.

"That won't wash, Wes. I went down and checked that brand and it was clearly a re-brand over ours. You've been stealing our cattle and telling us we were losing them in the black mud. I'm truly disappointed in you, Wes."

Baggett's eyes slowly narrowed to mere slits and his words took on a bite.

"Disappointed...I've been disappointed. Ever since I went to work for you I've busted my hump; and for what? Thirty five dollars a month, a lousy bed in a freezing bunkhouse in the winter and an oven in the summer, and three meals a day, and you're disappointed in me.

"I watched your boys blow more money in one trip to town than I make in a whole month. I see them wearing nice fancy duds on Sunday when I've got two shirts to my name. I see the women they have hanging on their arms compared to the ones I can manage to latch onto and you're disappointed. I saw my chance and took it, so what?" Baggett said venomously.

"You sure never let on that it bothered you; not that it would have mattered, mind you," John said evenly. "My boys earn every dollar they make. Sure I pay them more than I do the hired hands because they're my sons. I know my boys, and none of them would ever steal from me or anyone else; in fact, I would stake my life on them never stealing.

"In case you are interested, Miller is broken up, but he's going to pull through, so the doctor says. The man you shot wasn't so lucky. You'll be standing trial for murder, Wes. I hope you can afford a good lawyer, otherwise you may be in for a long drop with a short rope around your neck."

"They haven't gotten me to trial yet, and they sure haven't hanged me. I'll worry about a lawyer when I think I really need one," Wes spat out the words.

"I guess I've said all I came to say. I'm sorry for you, Wes, I really am," John said sincerely.

"Keep your sympathy for your sons; you'll need it."

John looked at Baggett for a moment and then asked one final question, "Wes, did you put Logan up to shooting AJ?"

"No...I put him up to shooting BJ. He's the one we wanted to get even with. When he fired Selman we saw our chance."

"My God, man, why?"

"BJ was getting a little too close to finding out what we were up to although he didn't know it. He was within two hundred yards of the spot where we were hiding the cattle, and fortunately none of them were bawling. We had to take action before he found us out."

John shook his head, turned and walked to the door that separated the sheriff's office from the cells. He started to say something, but instead just glanced down and walked out.

"Sheriff, I've got to get word to Brian that he's after the wrong man. Baggett just admitted to me that he and Miller were responsible for the shooting of AJ, but said it was intended for Brian," John said with a frown.

"Do you have any idea where Brian might be?"

"He said that Selman had talked about a girl in San Antonio. He figured that was where he would head for," John replied.

"I'll send a telegram to the sheriff down there and have him be on the lookout for Brian. He can pass the word along about Baggett. I just hope Brian hasn't gone through there already."

John smiled gratefully, "Me too. Thanks."

John looked at the sheriff, "That sure isn't the same man my family took in. How'd he cover up his feelings all this time?"

"If I could tell you that, John, I could tell you how the criminal's mind works. They don't think like normal people. They run things through a different mind set than we do. We can look at a hammer and see it as a carpentry tool; they look at it and see something to bash a person's head in with."

"I guess you're right. It's sad but true. When will the trial be held, do you know yet?"

"In about five days. We've got a judge coming through here then."

"They were either brazen or outright stupid to sell those cattle in town. Didn't they think word would get back to us?"

"Hey, thieves can be some of the dumbest people in the world," the sheriff grinned.

"I guess they can at that," John agreed and then added, "We'll be here for the trial, that's for sure. Add shooting AJ to the charges against him. I was surprised at how willingly he handed over that bit of information. I wonder why?"

"Maybe he doesn't want to die with that on his conscience. I've heard some damning confessions in my years as a sheriff when someone is facing the hangman's noose. They don't want to die with those sins hanging over them, I guess."

"The way he talked he doesn't plan on sticking around here for long," John said and then paused, "I'll bet you have heard some doozies all right. Well, I'd better get back out to the ranch."

"Give my regards to Loretta and AJ. I was glad to hear how well he's doing," the sheriff said with a grin.

"Thanks, I'll do that. I wish I could reach BJ and tell him to let Selman go; the man's innocent."

"Have you heard anything from him yet?"

"Not a word. Maybe in another few days, I hope," John said as he opened the door.

"Yeah, let's hope. I'll shoot that telegram off to San Antone, right away," the sheriff replied.

Fort Griffin

The cavalry telegrapher hurriedly jotted down the urgent message that came over the wire. When he'd finished receiving the message he tapped out his response; then tore off the sheet from the message pad.

"Corporal Hawkins, come in here," the sergeant yelled.

"Yes Sergeant," the corporal said rounding the corner.

"Get this message to the major fast. He'll want to know about this," the sergeant ordered.

"Yes, sir," the corporal said grabbing the message and rushing out of the telegraph office.

The major read the message and frowned at the news he read. Looking up at the corporal who had delivered the telegram he snapped an order.

"Corporal, go and get Captain Wainwright and be quick about it. Tell him I want to see him immediately. And, if he's with my daughter; ...well, just tell him to get his butt over here."

"In those exact words, Sir," the corporal asked questioningly?

"In those exact words; now get going," the major snapped.

The corporal found the captain in the first sergeant's office and told him what the major had said. Captain

John Wainwright reported immediately to the major and received his orders.

"Captain, we just got word that the Indians who have been attacking settlers and travelers is in fact the Black Jack Haggerty gang. They've donned Indian garb and made it look like the Kiowa or Comanche were pulling the raids. The good news is that they're on the run now and headed our way. I want you to take a detachment and intercept them."

"Yes sir, and where would that interception take place," the captain asked?

"Right here," the major said as he pointed to a large map of Texas.

He put his finger on a line that intersected at the Sackett Ranch. The captain, being familiar with that area, commented.

"That's the Sackett ranch, sir. Are you sure you want us to engage the gang there?"

"If I know John Sackett it will be like having a second wave at your disposal. Yes, I want you to engage the gang there; but I want you to beat them to the ranch and be waiting when they arrive. According to the telegram you'll have to make good time, but you can do it."

"I'll gather my men and be on the move within the hour, sir," the captain said.

"Within the half hour, Captain," the major said firmly.

'Within the half hour it is, Sir," the captain said with a grin.

12

The detachment of troops rode hard, arriving at the Sackett ranch just as John Sackett was returning from Abilene. The captain filled John in on what was about to take place and John sent a rider to round up all his ranch hands and have them meet at the main house.

The captain positioned his troopers around the area, keeping them well hidden and out of sight. Now all they could do was wait; wait and hope the message had been right as to where the other contingent of troops were driving the outlaw gang.

They didn't have to wait long. The gang rode over the crest of a hill that looked down on the Sackett ranch house. The leader, Black Jack Haggerty, raised his hand and called the fourteen riders he led to a halt.

"What is it, Jack," one of the men called out?

"Supplies and fresh horses," Jack replied, and then yelled, "Go in yelling and shooting. Shoot anything that moves, but the horses."

The riders kicked their mounts into a full gallop down the hillside towards the Sackett ranch. When they drew near to the main house they began to give Rebel yells and started firing towards the house and barn. Suddenly the entire area exploded with gunfire as the cavalry troops opened fire from their places of concealment. Gang members began to fall from their saddles and utter confusion broke out amongst the outlaw gang.

"Trap," Haggerty yelled out, "Get out of here."

The gang, which was by this time reduced to eight, turned and rode away from the ranch house, firing at the cavalry troopers who gave chase. The gang was forced to retreat in the same direction from which they'd come, which meant they were headed back towards the other contingent of troopers from Ft. McKavett.

By the time the Sackett wranglers arrived at the ranch the melee was over. John had them remain at the ranch, however, just in case the outlaws should double back. They couldn't double back, however, because the gang was hemmed in by the two detachments and cut down to merely two remaining gang members; Black Jack Haggerty and Four Fingers Jordan. They headed north to try and make it to the Oklahoma border.

No harm had come to any of the Sackett family and John was the only one who had been forced to fire a shot. It made for a lot of excitement, but no major damage to the Sackett house or anyone inside.

Laredo, Texas

Brent Sackett looked at his cards and then tossed a sawbuck on the pile of money in the middle of the table.

"I call," he said casually.

"Aces and eights," the man across from him smiled as he showed two pair.

"Hmm, they call that a dead man's hand," Brent said as he fiddled with his cards.

"Well ... come on, let's see what you got," the man said impatiently.

"Just hold on fella. I'll tell you what I'm willing to do," Brent said with a slight smile. "We'll split the pot, how's that?"

The man frowned, "What do you mean, 'split the pot', I'm not going to split the pot. Oh, that means you can't beat my two pair," he grinned.

"Not necessarily. Hey, I'm in a good mood and I thought I'd help you out a little, that's all. You've been losing all night long, so I'm offering to give you some of your money back."

"You're crazy. I won and you're trying to weasel out of holding a losing hand," the man said with a grin and then turned serious, "No, I won't split no pot with you. Let's see your cards."

"Okay, you boys heard me offer to split with him," Brent said looking at the other players.

"Yeah, we heard," they all agreed.

"Okay, here they are," Brent said and tossed three deuces onto the table and then added, "And if that isn't enough here are a couple of kings to go along with them."

The man's neck turned beet red as he looked at the full house Brent had laid out. He glared across the table at Sackett for several seconds. Everyone at the table could feel the tension mount. Brent looked at the man with a steady gaze but didn't speak.

Finally he broke the silence, "Are you going to deal or just sit there admiring me?"

"I'm broke and you know it," the man snapped.

"Then I guess you'd better move and let someone with money sit down. We can't win money from someone who doesn't have any," Brent said and chuckled.

"I think you're cheating," the man finally said.

111

The table grew deathly silent as the men all looked at the man and then at Brent to see his reaction. Brent had been looking down at the money he was arranging in front of him, but slowly raise his head to look at the man across the table from him.

"You've got five seconds to apologize for that remark," he said.

"I'll say it again; I think you're cheating."

Brent clenched his teeth as his forehead tightened from the frown that now formed.

"Your times up," he said just before the roar of the .44 erupted from under the table.

The bullet caught the man in the midsection and knocked him back in his chair, which turned over and spilled the man onto the floor. He didn't know what hit him; he was stone cold dead.

The saloon girl who had been hanging over Brent screamed and ran towards the bar. The men seated at the table jumped to their feet which caused Brent to level his gun at them.

"If any of you are this man's friends you'd better not go for your gun," he said loudly.

"We don't even know the man," someone said rapidly.

Someone else commented quickly, "The sheriff ain't going to like this, friend. If I was you I'd high tail it across the border before the sheriff gets here."

"You saw that it was self defense; why should I leave," Brent said casually.

"If you knew our sheriff, you'd know why," the man went on.

Brent looked at the men and then smiled coyly, "Well if I'm going to have to head for Mexico I'll need a little traveling money. So that being the case I guess I'll just take the money that's sitting in front of each of you."

The men gave one another a quick look before looking back to see if he was serious. The way he held his pistol told them that he was, in deed, very serious.

"Toss your guns behind the bar and be quick about it," Brent said. The men didn't hesitate in following his order.

Brent gathered the player's money together and dumped it onto a table covered with a table cloth. He bundled the money up and began backing towards the saloon door. He reached the door and stopped. The men were poised to spring towards the bar to get their guns and follow him so he decided to cause a little pandemonium before leaving.

There was a kerosene lantern in the window that illuminated a small area. Sackett grabbed the lantern and slung it down into the doorway. The lantern instantly burst into flames, thus cutting them off from the front entrance. The men he'd just robbed forgot about him for the time being and scrambled away from the fire.

Brent ran to the hitching rail and swung into the saddle. He kicked his horse up and headed for the bridge that crossed over the Rio Grande into Mexico. He could hear the screams and shouts of 'fire, fire' as he rode away.

Sackett wasn't crazy about staying in Mexico for any length of time. He'd heard, however, that a man could live like a king just about anywhere in Mexico if he had several thousand dollars. He had that and more, so why not head on down to Monterrey and see if what he'd heard was true. After all, it was only about a three and half days ride. The problem was it was a hundred and fifty miles in Mexico. That meant it could be extremely dangerous due to the bandits that roamed the hills.

Brent decided to stop in Nuevo Laredo and see if he might hook up with another person with whom he could make the trip to Monterrey. After all, Nuevo Laredo was loaded with men who'd crossed the border one step ahead of the law. It didn't take him long to find just two such men.

The small bar had a Mexican guitar player and a couple of plump Mexican women cozying up to the patrons for whatever they could get from them. There were several Americano men in the bar who eyed the new arrival with wary looks.

Brent ordered a bottle of Tequila and sat down at a table that had one leg a touch shorter than the other three. He frowned as he wobbled the table back and forth. Looking down he saw which leg was the problem and took a sheet of cigarette paper out of his pocket and folded it several times. While he was bending over to slip the paper under the leg, he saw the two pair of boots walk up and stop at his table.

Sackett looked up into the faces of two men wearing a week's growth of beard. They both had their thumbs tucked into the buckles on their gun belts to show they weren't a threat. When he looked up, the taller of the two spoke.

"Your last name wouldn't be Sackett by any chance would it?"

Brent tensed as he sat upright in his chair, his hand moving close to his pistol.

"That all depends on who's asking and why," he responded.

"You sure look like the BJ Sackett I served with during the War. The name's Nagle, Charlie Nagle, from Illinois."

"No, you were a little too far north for me," Brent replied, but taking special notice of the name.

"Oh...I'm sorry. I didn't mean you no harm. You Southern boys sure put up one heck of a fight, I'll give you that," the man grinned.

"Yeah, we fought back, but not good enough, obviously; you boys care for a drink," Brent offered?

"Say, that's mighty kind of you. We don't mind if we do," Nagle said as the two sat down.

Sackett looked towards the bar and called out, "Two more glasses over here."

"This here is Willard Winkler; he doesn't talk too much because of a speech problem," Nagle said.

"Say Willard," Brent said as he extended his hand to the two men. "My name is...Dan Johnson."

"Man, I tell you, Dan; you could pass for the identical twin brother of the man I served with, I swear. His name was Brian Sackett, but he went by BJ," Nagle said.

"Yeah, that's what you said. I guess we've all got someone who looks like us out there somewhere," Brent replied.

"I pity the poor soul who has to wear my mug around with him," Nagle laughed just as one of the women walked up and set two empty glasses on the table.

"Buy me a drink, Senor," she said with a smile that exposed a missing front tooth.

"Nope," Brent said coldly.

She looked at him and threw her head back as she stormed off back towards the bar.

"Cow," Brent said under his breath before addressing his next question to Nagle. "What brings you boys to this stink hole, anyway," Brent asked?

Nagle cast a quick glance at Winkler before answering, "We got into a little scrape up north around Dallas. We had to make a beeline for the border. We just crossed over last night. What about you?"

Sackett grinned, "Same thing. I caught a man cheating in a card game and shot him; he turned out to be the brother of the local sheriff. I had to scram out of there as fast as I could with the law one step behind me. I just rode in today," Brent lied.

"We were thinking about heading down to Mexico City. We hear a man can live like a king down there if he's got the money," Nagle said with a grin. "Where are you headed?"

"I'm on my way to Monterrey; and you can live just as high on the hog there without having to travel near as far," Brent said and then added, "And a man can live like a king just about anywhere...if he's got the money."

"Yeah, I guess that was a dumb statement, but, hey...I'm full of dumb statements," Nagle said with a loud laugh.

"Maybe we could hook up and ride together. I'm not too crazy about traveling through Mexico alone. I've heard stories about the gangs of Mexican bandits that ride these parts. Three guns are a lot better than one," Brent said, getting right to the point.

"That's exactly what I was telling Willard. So when were you planning on pulling out," Nagle asked?

"I was thinking about tomorrow morning. I sure don't cotton to hanging around this place any longer than I have to."

"Have you ever been to Monterrey?"

"Nope, but I've heard from those that have that the Tequila is great and the women are beautiful."

"Now you're talking my language," Nagle grinned and downed his glass of Tequila.

Across the room the woman who had brought the glasses to Sackett's table was talking to a rough looking hombre with a scar that passed from his forehead, across one eye and down to his cheek. He eyed the three men with an angry scowl that seemed to fit naturally.

She spoke to him in Spanish as they stood there. Brent just happened to glance their way and when he did the woman turned her back towards him. The rough looking man, however, never took his eyes off the three men.

"I think we have someone interested in us," Brent said to Nagle.

"Oh, and who would that be?"

"That hombre over at the end of the bar," Sackett said with a nod of his head.

Nagle looked towards the man and then back at Brent, "Now that is one ugly man. Do you think he's eyeing us for any particular reason?"

"I'd think so. He may be the woman's protector and she told him I was rude to her. Looking around this room, I'd say the Gringos are a little outnumbered, wouldn't you?"

"Yep, sure looks that way. Maybe we ought to drink up and get out of here," Nagle said as Winkler grinned and looked around at the people in the bar.

"We c-c-could t-take –'em. There a-a-ain't that m-m-many of 'em," Willard said.

Brent looked at the stuttering man with a slight grin, "Is he serious?"

"Let's just say he loves a good squabble. He hated to see the War end," Nagle said with an affirming nod.

"Let's get some supplies for the trip, what do you say," Brent suggested. "I want to head out at first light in the morning."

"Let's do it," Nagle agreed.

As they walked out of the small bar, Brent gave the man with the scar another quick look and saw the man was still watching them. He was pleased that he'd found two men to travel with so easily, but didn't like the feeling he got from the scar faced man. At least they'd be leaving Laredo early the next morning.

13

Brian (BJ) Sackett rode to the top of a hill that allowed him a good view of the trail beyond. He had managed to pick up Selman's trail again and could see that the man was headed for Crystal City.

After scanning the horizon he kicked up his horse and moved on down the slope. His horse pulled at the reins to stretch out its gait, but Sackett kept a tight rein on the spirited animal.

He was about three miles from Crystal City when he met a man and woman in a buckboard who had been to town for supplies. As he neared them he noticed the man eye him suspiciously. The man's eyes suddenly widened and he said something to his wife who also viewed BJ with a curious look.

Sackett tipped his hat to the couple, but got nothing in return, nothing but the same curious stares. He wondered what they saw so interesting in him, but shrugged it off at first. When he had traveled about fifty yards he turned in the saddle and looked back. The couple had pulled their wagon to a stop and was watching him.

BJ covered the distance in less than thirty minutes. He brought his horse to a walk as he moved down the town's main street. People walking along the boardwalk as well as those he met on horseback, or in wagons, gave him the same curious stares the couple he'd met earlier had.

"I sure must be a sight, the way folks are eyeing me," he said to his horse.

Just then he saw a man and a boy walk out of the general store. Again, when they saw him they stopped dead in their tracks. The man actually glared at BJ and then said something to the boy, who instantly took off running down the street.

BJ reined up in front of a small building that bore a sign that simply read, "Bar." He stepped down off his horse and tied the reins to the hitching rail; looking around at more passersby, he drew more suspicious stares.

He shook his head as he dusted himself off and walked into the bar. Upon entering the saloon, three men standing at the bar looked towards him and then moved aside to give him plenty of room. BJ eyed them as he stepped up to the bar.

"Howdy," he said with a slight grin.

The men nodded slightly; their eyes wide, but no one spoke. The bartender moved up cautiously to where he stood. His questioning look was all BJ could take.

"Why is everyone staring at me like I've got two heads," he asked?

"You mean you don't know," the bartender replied?

"No, I don't know. What is it with folks in this town, anyway?"

"If you don't know that then I sure can't enlighten you any," the man said cautiously.

BJ shook his head in wonderment and then said, "Give me a beer. I can get a beer here, can't I.?"

"Sure thing Brent," the bartender replied and started to turn away.

"What did you call me," BJ asked?

"Brent, Brent Sackett...that is your name isn't it?"

"Sackett, yes; Brent...no," BJ replied, his eyes now widened by the name he'd just heard.

Before the bartender could respond the door to the bar burst opened and two men armed with sawed off shotguns rushed in. BJ spun around at the sudden entrance of the men, but didn't go for his gun when he saw them leveling their scatterguns at him.

"Don't move, Sackett. Just give me a reason and I'll cut you in two," the man with a badge that read 'Sheriff' said angrily.

"Whoa Sheriff; easy there...I don't know what's going on here, but I'm not a part of it," BJ said holding his hands out towards the sheriff to show he wasn't reaching for his gun.

"You've got more gall than any one I've ever seen, Sackett. You gun down the sheriff and then just ride back into town as though nothing happened? Come on...you're going to jail."

"I've never been in this town before, Sheriff. I just rode in," BJ said and then recalled what the bartender had called him. "Wait a minute...he called me Brent Sackett. Is that who everyone thinks I am?"

"Don't try and talk your way out of this Brent. Come on, let's go," the sheriff said with a wave of the gun.

"My name is Brian Sackett," BJ said as he moved away from the bar. "I had a twin brother by the name of Brent, but he was killed in the War."

"Yeah, yeah, tell it to the judge when you go to court...if you ever get to court," the sheriff snapped.

"What do you mean by that?"

"You killed a well liked, well respected man when you killed Ben Cates. Some of the citizens may just want to speed justice up a little and lynch you."

"I never heard the name Ben Cates, and I told you I'm not Brent Sackett. I can clear all this up if you'll give me the chance," BJ said as he got to the opened door. "In fact, he can clear it all up right now," he said and pointed off to the right side of the bar.

The sheriff and deputy both took a split second to glance in the direction BJ had pointed, which gave him just enough time to make a desperate move. He instantly shoved the sheriff into the unsuspecting deputy and jumped through the open doorway.

Because the deputy had both hammers back on his shotgun, he involuntarily pulled the trigger, firing both barrels into the floor. The sheriff spun around and fired both barrels of his shotgun through the now closed door, leaving a gaping hole in the middle of it.

Before anyone knew what was happening, BJ snapped open the door again and rushing inside, grabbed up a chair near the door and hit the sheriff over the head with it; buckling the lawman's knees. The deputy was trying to find more shells for the spent ones in his shotgun, but when he saw the reemergence of Sackett, dropped the gun and threw up his hands.

BJ quickly turned and ran out of the bar to the hitching rail where he untied his horse and swung into the saddle. BJ spun the horse around and the animal quickly hit a full run down the main street. He was about one hundred and fifty yards away when the first of three gunshots rang out.

The bullets missed, but BJ saw the dust kick up off to his right. He leaned out over the racing horse's neck, making himself as small a target as he possibly could. He didn't raise himself up until he had cleared the city limits.

He knew that there would be a posse on his trail and not knowing the territory knew they would have an advantage. He was sure he could outrun his pursuers for a ways, but knew also that his horse needed rest after his long trek. There had to be a place where he could hide and give his horse a rest; but where?

BJ looked over his shoulder and was pleased that he could not see any sign of a posse. He knew there would be one, but figured it was taking them awhile to form it. That was time that he could use to his advantage. When he saw a large dried out, broken branch lying beneath a tree he had an idea.

He reined his horse to a halt next to the limb. Grabbing his lariat he quickly tied it to the butt end of the branch and kicked up his horse again, dragging the limb along behind them. The limb kicked up a lot of dust, but did a fairly good job of removing his horse's tracks. He was fully aware that this action would only slow the posse down momentarily, but knew he had to do something in order to give his horse a breather.

Sackett slowed his pace as much as he dared, but constantly eyed the horizon behind him for dust kicked up by the posse. He had traveled about a mile when he spotted another means by which to throw the posse off his trail. It was a good sized herd of cattle grazing on open range.

He reined his horse towards the herd and slowed his pace so as not to stampede the grazing cattle. Riding into the middle of the herd he unloosed the end of the rope used to drag the tree branch from around the saddle horn and extended the loop. He rode up alongside a steer and tossed the loop over its head. He then slowly maneuvered his horse to the side of the herd.

BJ cast a look around the area and then drew his pistol and held it into the air. With a mighty whoop he fired his gun several times and continued to whoop and holler until he'd spooked the herd into a full out stampede.

Knowing the stampeding herd would remove all traces of his horse's hoof prints he took the lead. His horse could easily stay ahead of the cattle and he would be able to peel off at anytime and not have to worry about the posse picking up his tracks any too soon. After a good half mile he did just that.

Upon topping a small rise he looked back at the herd and smiled. Now he would be able to walk his horse and give it a much needed rest. It was now that he could focus on what the sheriff and the bartender had said.

They had mistaken him for Brent Sackett. Could it be that Brent was alive and really hadn't been killed in the War Between the States? The odds of there being another Brent Sackett were too great; and especially when you consider the fact that an entire town had thought him to be Brent.

Now he was presented with another dilemma; if Brent was alive, he was a wanted man. Brian remembered that his twin had always had a hot temper. He could recall incidents as kids when Brent would light into some other kid for the least out of line remark. But, to think of his brother as a killer was hard to do.

BJ thought back to what some of his fellow Union soldiers had said after a hard battle and it gave him cause to wonder. A few of them told him and others when they would be sitting around in camp, that the rush they felt when in battle had them addicted to violence. They lived for the moments when their life was on the line and it was kill or be killed. It had never had that effect on him, however; in fact, he had hated those moments when he was forced to take another's life.

Brent Sackett took the lead as he and his new found traveling companions rode out of Nuevo Laredo headed for Monterrey. He felt a lot better about siding with two more guns while passing through the territory they'd have to travel.

What Brent didn't know was that they did not leave Nuevo Laredo unnoticed. The scar faced Mexican from the bar had kept one of his gang members watching them from the time they'd left the small bar. As soon as they had began packing up that morning for their trip, the man posted to watch them reported to the gang leader as to their intention.

The Mexican gang stayed a good distance behind the three Americans as they headed south towards Monterrey. The leader of the gang, Jorge Santos, sent his best scout ahead to keep an eye on the three Americans and leave a clearly marked trail for the gang to follow. They didn't want to make their presence known too soon. When the time was right they'd catch up, kill and rob the men they suspected of carrying many US dollars on their person.

Santos led a gang of about fifteen men; small in size when compared to some of the other gangs, but just as violent. The gang traveled along the Rio Grande and would make raids on the US side and then flee back across the Rio Grande to safety in Mexico.

One of Santos favorite spots to set up ambushes in this area was the Rio Salado, a river where travelers liked to make camp. Three men traveling by themselves would offer no trouble to the gang; or so it seemed to the bandit leader.

Sackett kept a wary eye on the trail behind them. He had the distinct feeling that they were being followed, but had not actually seen anyone as yet. Still, the feeling persisted. Finally he felt he had to call it to the others attention.

"Say, Nagle; I think I'll drop back and make sure no one is following us. I don't know why, but I have a feeling someone is and I don't like it. I'll pull off and wait to see if someone shows up. You boys just keep on the way we're going. If no one is following I'll catch up."

Nagle looked back in the direction from which they had come and simply nodded his agreement. Winkler looked disinterested in the conversation and never took his eyes off the horizon in front of them. As Brent reined his horse around to take up a position along the trail, but out of sight, Nagle commented.

"Be careful, Johnson," Nagle said.

"What," Brent said; forgetting for a moment that he'd told the two his name was Dan Johnson. Catching his near mistake he said quickly, "Oh, yeah, thanks."

Brent rode back down the trail about two hundred yards and then reined his horse off to his right to the crest of a small hill that had a cluster of rocks at the top. He rode around in back of the boulders and dismounted. He pulled his rifle from the scabbard and took up a position that would give him a good view of the trail below. He figured he'd wait about fifteen minutes to make sure no one was following them. As it turned out he didn't have to wait long at all.

Within five minutes from the time he'd taken up his position in the rocks Brent saw a lone rider top the rise off to his left. The rider kicked his horse into an easy lope as he moved down the trail checking the ground for tracks as he rode.

Brent knew the way the man scoured the trail that he was definitely tracking the three of them. Sackett didn't believe for a moment that the man was by himself. He grinned as he watched the man draw near to where he lay in wait.

The rider stopped his horse and peered down at the ground. He raised his head and squinted as he looked down the trail in the direction the three horses had gone. He kicked his horse up and started to ride on when the crack of the rifle shot sounded, knocking the man from the saddle.

Brent ran back to where his horse was and mounted up. Figuring that the man was not alone, Sackett wasted no time riding to where he had downed the Mexican. The man's horse was standing a few feet from where the man had fallen; the Mexican was no where to be seen now, though.

Brent snapped his head around looking in all directions for the man he knew he had hit. Then he saw the drops of blood on the ground. The man was bleeding badly; probably gut shot. Brent began to follow the trail of blood, while keeping a wary eye on the trail behind him.

If this man was a member of a gang of Mexican bandits the others wouldn't be too far off, Brent thought. He had to hurry and find the man in order to hide his body from the gang. He didn't want them to know that he was on to them. He just hoped they were not within earshot of the rifle's report.

The trail of blood wound around some brush and down to a small creek. Sackett moved slowly, his pistol in his hand, having put his rifle in its scabbard. He knew that if the man was gut shot he was still a very dangerous man indeed.

Sackett saw that the drops of blood went to a large thicket. The man was somewhere around the brush. Brent dismounted and began to move closer to the large thicket. He glanced down at the droplets and knew that the man must be getting weak from his loss of blood.

The clicking of the hammer on the wounded man's pistol got Brent's full attention. Then a single gunshot rang out. Brent dropped to one knee; his gun moving back and forth waiting for the next shot to ring out. Suddenly he sprang to his feet and hurried around the brush where he found the Mexican man lying on the ground, dead.

A gunshot wound to the head said it all. Brent had shot the man in the stomach; therefore, the man knew he was not going to make it. Rather than die a slow agonizing death the man had taken his own life.

Brent hurriedly went through the man's pockets and found three, twenty dollar gold pieces. He gathered up the man's guns and climbed back into the saddle. He rode back to where the bandit's horse had stopped and was feeding on a small patch of grass. The loose horse didn't move as Brent rode up next to it and grabbed the bridle reins. He kicked his horse into a gallop and caught up with Nagle and Winkler.

"What was that shooting about back there," Nagle asked?

"Bandit; we'd better get a move on because the rest of the gang is not far behind," Brent said as he looked back down the trail behind him.

"Are you sure," Nagle questioned?

"I'm sure."

Nagle frowned, "Did you see them?"

"No, I didn't see them ... but I know they're there. Let's pick up the pace and put some distance between us."

"Are you sure he was a bandit," Nagle asked with a frown.

"Look, if you want to believe the man was a circuit preacher down here to save souls, for crying out loud, you go right ahead. I told you what the man was and I'm not sticking around here to be an easy target for the gang. You and that half wit you're traveling with can do as you please," Brent said and reined his horse around Nagle.

Nagle and Winkler watched Sackett ride away and finally Nagle looked at Winkler and spoke, "The man was a bandit."

Winkler grinned, "A b-b-bandit," he said agreeably.

With that the two men kicked their horses up and caught up with Sackett.

Jorge Santos, leader of the Mexican gang known to locals as, 'the Jackals', galloped ahead of his men as they followed Brent Sackett and his two traveling companions. When they reached the area where Brent had shot the gang's scout he held up his hand for them to halt. After scanning the area, Santos climbed down off his horse and searched the ground.

He tracked the horses' hoof prints as well as the boot prints made by both his man and the Gringo. He said something in Spanish to his men and they began riding around looking for any sign of their gang member.

Santos followed the boot prints and the drops of blood to the brush where the scout's body had been hidden. He called his men to where he was and knelt over the body as the gang members rode up around him.

Santos stared down at the body for several long seconds before finally mounting up again. One of his men gave him a questioning look and then asked in English.

"Aren't you going to bury him?"

Santos looked at the man through dead, uncaring eyes, "Why, he is dead. He will not know what happens to his body. Come, let's ride. Making the Gringos pay will settle the score."

The gang picked up the trail of the three Americans and held a steady pace to cut down the distance separating them. Now more than ever, Santos wanted to catch the men. The man who had been killed was a cousin of Santos and he would not rest until he had avenged his death.

14

Black Jack Haggerty, along with Frank "Four Fingers" Jordan, rode into the small town of Red Springs. The two rider's horses were lathered and winded; walking along with their heads held low due to their fatigue.

"We'll get fresh horses at the livery stable," Haggerty said to his right hand man.

"I hate to get rid of my horse. She's been a good animal," Jordan said with a frown.

"These horses will just slow us down. They're too tired to be of much use to us. No, we'll get two fresh mounts and keep moving until we reach Oklahoma Territory," Haggerty snapped.

"What are you planning on using for money, Jack, have you thought about that?"

"Yeah, Frank I have; see that bank over there," Haggerty said nodding in the direction of the small Cattlemen's Bank off to their right. "That's where we'll get the money."

Jordan smiled as he eyed the small bank. It looked like an easy bank to rob. But then, you never could be too certain about how these small town banks might be.

Some of them were better protected than the bigger ones in larger cities. This bank, however, did not have a well protected bank.

"Well, at least we won't have to dress up like Indians for this job," Jordan grinned.

"Yeah...There's the livery stable up ahead. Now, you let me do the talking. I've done a lot of horse trading in my day."

"Did you make the deal on that nag you're riding now," Four Fingers asked with a silly grin?

"This horse stayed ahead of that crow bait thing you're riding," Black Jack replied.

"I was holding her back," Four Fingers answered back quickly.

"That's the first time I've seen a man take a quirt to a horse to try and hold it back."

The two rode up to the livery stable and stepped down, stretching and twisting to get the kinks out after their long ride. The old man who ran the livery stable walked up to them and looked at the two lathered horses.

"I'd say those horses have covered a lot of territory and in short order," the old man said.

"Now here's a man with an eagle's eye," Haggerty said, "What gave it away?"

The old man chuckled at the comeback as he patted Haggerty's horse's neck and then added, "You wouldn't be interested in trading horses would you?"

"We might be, if we could get a good enough deal. What have you got in the corral over there?"

"I've got a couple of good ones, but they're not for sale or trade."

"Then there's no point in us talking. These are good horses, just winded after out running a band of renegade Indians. We'll just put them up for a couple of days in your stable here and they'll be raring to go," Haggerty said as he turned his back giving the impression the trading was over.

"Now, wait a minute; why don't you take a look in the corral and see if there's some horse flesh that strikes your fancy. We might still be able to do business," the old man said as he checked Haggerty's horse's teeth.

"I guess it wouldn't hurt to look; come on Frank," he said to Jordan.

The two men walked over to the corral and each grabbed a halter rope draped over the top rail. They immediately saw the two horses they would be willing to trade for and walked over to them. They each clicked the rope snap into the horse's halter and walked them around checking to see if they showed any signs of lameness. Satisfied that the horses were sound of hoof and legs, they checked the horses' teeth to determine their age.

"I'll take this one," Haggerty said firmly.

"Here too," Jordan agreed.

They led the horses to the rail and tied the halter ropes to one of the rails and then went back to where the old man was going over their mounts' condition.

"What about those two horses over at the rail, old hoss," Haggerty asked?

The old man looked that way and shook his head negatively, 'Nope, sorry boys; those two aren't for trade."

"They're the only two worth having," Haggerty snapped with a frown.

"Oh, if you want to give a little to boot, we might make a deal," the old man said evenly.

"I'll give you a little boot...a boot in the...how much are you talking here?"

"Oh, I dunno...let's say fifty dollars a piece," the old man said rubbing the back of his neck.

"Well you crazy old coot, you must be out of your mind if you think we'd give you that kind of money plus our mounts," Haggerty said angrily.

"That's my offer, take it or leave it," the old man said.

"I'm glad you said that," Haggerty said, having looked around the area and not seeing anyone with prying eyes.

He whipped out his pistol and hit the old man over the head with it, knocking the old man unconscious. He grabbed the old fella as he started to fall and he and Jordan hurriedly carried him inside his office.

"We'll, tie and gag him. No one will find him until we've done what we have to do," Haggerty said as they laid the old guy on the office floor.

"Remind me never to do any horse trading with you, Jack," Jordan said with a laugh. "You're a tough negotiator."

"Hey, I wouldn't have done this if he had been more reasonable. I was thinking an even trade," Haggerty said acting somewhat incensed by the whole thing. "Tie him up and I'll saddle the horses," he then added.

"Where do you want me to stow him once I'm done?"

"Over behind those sacks of feed. No one will see him if they come in for any reason. Hurry up; we've got to get out of here before someone does come along."

Jordan finished with the old man just as Haggerty was finishing the saddling of the two fresh horses. They mounted up and rode away from the livery stable just as a stagecoach rounded the bend; it was headed into town and the Red Springs Bank.

The coach passed the two men leaving them in a cloud of dust. Haggerty looked at Jordan and grinned.

"Looks like our timing was perfect, Frank," Jack said.

"Yeah, bringing a little more money to the bank for us," Jordan grinned.

"We'll wait until they get it inside and hit before they leave."

"Why, that means there'll be another gun in the bank...the guy riding shotgun," Jordan questioned?

"I don't want to take the chance that the coach might be taking money out of the bank, Frank. There may well be a transfer of money to another bank."

"Oh, I guess that's why you're the boss, huh."

"That among other things," Jack replied.

They tied their horses across the street from the bank because of the coach being in front of it. They moved to the corner of a building and waited until the guard and driver had unloaded the strongbox from the coach's foot well.

The two bandits timed their arrival at the bank's front door so they entered right behind the guard and driver. Once inside Jack didn't waste anytime; he shot the guard and driver in the back, while Jordan shot down a clerk and aimed his pistol at the bank's president who had rushed out of his office. The one woman customer in the bank screamed and then crumpled to the floor in a dead faint.

"Open the safe," Jack called to the president, and then added quickly, "You," he said to the other clerk, "open this box."

The bank president started to argue, but when Black Jack cocked the hammer back on his pistol, he hurriedly grabbed the key and opened the strongbox.

"Do as they say, Ed," the president called to the teller. "They mean what they say."

Jordan moved over to the teller's window and opened the money drawer while the president opened the bank's safe and the teller was unlocking the strongbox. Jordan grinned when he saw the hundred dollar bills in the till.

"Hey, we've hit the jackpot here," Jordan said and looked towards Jack.

By looking away he gave the president a chance to grab the pistol the bank kept in the safe. The president pulled the pistol and turned it towards Jordan. Cocking the hammer back alerted Jordan.

The bandit moved quickly to one side and fired two quick shots, killing the president. Anger flashed across Black Jack's face and he looked quickly towards his partner, the president, and then back at the clerk. He shook his head and pulled the trigger, shooting the clerk down in cold blood.

Black Jack walked over to where the president lay and fired one more shot into the man's head. He hurriedly gathered up the money that remained in the safe and ran to help Jordan grab more from the strongbox.

"We've got to get out of here. Those shots will bring the law running," Haggerty snapped at Four Fingers as they shoved the money into some money bags they found under the teller's window.

They didn't get all the money, but certainly enough to make their robbery worthwhile. When they reached the front door a crowd of curious onlookers was already forming. The town had a sheriff, but no deputies.

Haggerty and Jordan ran across the street to where the horses were tied and sprang into the saddles. They slipped the drawstrings of the moneybags over the saddle horns so their gun hands would be free.

The local sheriff came running down the street towards the bank. He was carrying a shotgun, but no sidearm. Although he was out of range of the scattergun he fired at the two bandits anyway. Frank Jordan looked back and fired one shot that hit the lawman in the leg causing him to fall to the ground.

"Come on, forget him," Black Jack yelled out.

The two bandits reined their horses around and raced out of town heading north. A few more people took wild shots at the fleeing bandits, but missed. The horses the bandits had chosen were good. They both had good speed and handled well. The two had made good on their bank robbery.

15

Brian Sackett topped a high hill and started down the other side when he suddenly stopped. He peered down the hillside to a stagecoach road below. There was a man on foot with his saddle hoisted over one shoulder. It was too far to make out the identity of the man, but BJ felt sure he had caught up with Myron Selman.

Not wanting to alert Selman of his presence, BJ turned his mount into a draw that would conceal him all the way down the hill to the road. Once Selman saw him at that point it would be too late for him to make a stand; if the man was Selman.

The point where the draw reached the road left Sackett only twenty yards behind the man on foot. With everything being so dry, his horse kicked up a fair amount of dust which could alert the man of someone's presence. Walking with his back towards the draw, however, made it a little less likely that the dust would be noticed.

The man afoot stopped and twisted his foot from side to side. He had picked up a small rock in his boot and tried to work it to a point where it wouldn't hurt.

Thinking he had done so, he started walking again, but soon realized that the rock was still hurting him.

The man dropped his saddle and sat down on it to remove his boot. He had his foot hoisted up so he could pull the boot off when BJ rode out onto the stagecoach road. His sudden emergence startled the man, causing him to snap his head around to see who had just rode up onto the road.

BJ had his hand on his pistol as he peered down the road at the man who was sitting on his saddle. Sackett could see that the man was not Myron Selman. He slowly moved his hand away from his gun.

The man went ahead and removed his boot; turning it upside down and emptying the small rock onto the ground. He pulled the boot back on as BJ rode up to where he sat.

"Howdy," the man said.

"Say...what happened to your horse," BJ asked?

"I had a man hold me up. He took my horse, my rifle, and what money I had in my pocket. He didn't know about the ten dollars I keep tucked under my hat band, though. He said he needed my horse more than I did," the man said as he stood up.

"What did the man look like," BJ asked?

"He was close to six feet tall; a hundred sixty five or seventy pounds. He had sandy colored hair and was left handed; his holster was on his left side and he held his gun in his left hand," the man said thoughtfully.

The description fit Myron Selman.

"Did his horse give out on him," BJ asked?

"Yeah, he didn't say anymore than that he needed my horse more than I did, though. At least he left me my saddle; he kept his own."

"Are you from around here," BJ asked?

"No, I'm from Laredo. I was on my way back to the ranch where I work. It's going to take me a lot longer to get there now though," the man said shaking his head.

"I can help you out a little bit; at least to the next way station. You can probably catch a ride on a stagecoach the rest of the way," BJ said with a grin.

"Man I sure would appreciate it. Oh, yeah; there's one thing about that horse I forgot to mention. The horse was stolen from the ranch where I work. They caught the man who stole it and I took a stagecoach up to fetch it back to the ranch. If someone sees that brand who knows most of the cowhands from our ranch; they might just think that he stole the horse....which he did, huh," the man grinned.

BJ's ears pricked up at the news, "That's right he did. And you say the man headed in the same direction we're heading?"

"Yeah, unless he cut off the road after he got out of my sight. Boy, I tell you; my boss is going to be fit to be tied when I tell him the horse was stolen again."

"Climb aboard. How far is it to the next relay station anyway; do you know?"

"It's not more than three, maybe four miles," the man said as he climbed up behind BJ on the horse.

The ride to the relay station was actually less than three miles. Once there BJ told the man goodbye and kicked his horse into a nice easy lope. His next stop was Laredo.

Laredo, Texas

The sheriff of Laredo looked scornfully at the wounded Mexican woman and shook his head.

"Why won't you tell me who it was who shot you and your two brothers? Don't you want the man to be brought to justice?"

"I told you, Sheriff; the man wore a mask so we could not see his face," the woman lied as she lay in her bed where she was recovering from her wounds.

"Now I know better than that, Ramona. No one is going to come down here to rob anyone. I figure he stopped to spend some time with you and your brothers tried to rob him, am I right?"

"How could you say that about my dead brothers, Sheriff," Ramona snapped angrily.

"Oh, yeah I know; they were a couple of real saints. Listen, I'm surprised someone hadn't done this a long time ago. Now if you won't identify the man for me I can't do a thing for you. If he walks into my office I couldn't touch him because you won't give me a description of the man," the sheriff said honestly.

"If he ever comes back to Laredo, I will take care of him myself," Ramona said evenly, her eyes narrowing as she spoke.

"Yeah, and you'll wind up like your brothers; dead as a doornail," the sheriff said as he moved towards the door.

"Thank you, anyway, Sheriff," Ramona said forcing a smile.

"Yeah...you're welcome," the sheriff said and walked out of the small adobe house.

The sheriff went back to his office and started going through a stack of wanted posters. He hadn't looked at many when he suddenly grinned.

"I knew it, I knew it," he said as he eyed the brand new wanted poster with a photo of Brent Sackett under the words Wanted Dead or Alive for murdering the sheriff of Crystal City. The reward was for one thousand dollars.

To himself the sheriff stated, "I'll bet another thousand dollars to cover that reward money that he's not in town any more. No sir, he's long gone into Mexico."

Still, he wanted to prove to himself that the man in the wanted poster was not still in Laredo. He grabbed his sawed off shotgun and headed out to make the rounds of all the cantinas and saloons. He'd even make another trip to the houses of women for hire.

Now the sheriff had a photo to show folks and could watch their expression to see if they recognized the man, whether they said they did or not. This time around the sheriff picked up a lot more information on the man Brent Sackett.

BJ Sackett was only a day's ride out of Laredo and was riding headlong into a hornet's nest. Brent Sackett had created an explosive situation for his twin brother BJ and didn't even know it; not that it would have mattered; in fact, he couldn't have laid out a trap any better than the one he had, even if he'd tried. There was another surprise awaiting BJ in Laredo, also; Myron Selman.

Selman rode slowly down the main street of Laredo and eyed the town he had only visited one other time. He wondered if his cousin was still here since he had not heard from the man for some five years.

Seeing a familiar 'watering hole' he had frequented the last time he was here, he reined the horse he'd stolen towards the hitching rail in front of the small cantina, and stepped down. He walked into the bar and up to the counter. A grizzled looking bartender walked over and asked him what he wanted. Selman ordered a beer and some beans and tortillas.

As the bartender walked away a man standing at the other end of the approached Selman. The man wore two guns; one in a holster and another tucked under his belt. The man's eyes said he was someone you couldn't, or wouldn't turn your back on for a second. The scar on his neck added to the man's rugged appearance.

"You're standing in my spot," the man said, his eyes drooping badly due to the amount of Mescal he'd consumed.

"What," Selman asked with a frown.

"You are standing in my spot," the man repeated, slurring his words badly.

"You're drunk," Selman said angrily, trying to ignore him.

"If you don't move I'm going to kill you," the man went on as he walked up to within three feet of Selman.

"Look, I'm in no mood to put up with your mouth. Move on or I'll remove a few of those rotten teeth you have in your mouth," Selman growled.

The man started to reach for his gun, but Selman whipped his pistol out and hit the man over the head with it, and very hard. The man fell hard, hitting his head on the edge of the bar in the process. When he hit the floor he just lay there, motionless.

"What is going on here," the bartender called out from the small kitchen area of the cantina?

"Nothing...now; one of your customers got a little unruly is all," Selman called back to the man.

The bartender came around the bar from the kitchen to take a look at the man on the floor. When he rolled the man over and saw his face, his eyes widened.

"Ah chi wah-wah," the bartender said quietly as he tended to the man.

"You know this man," Selman asked?

"Oh, si, everyone knows this man in Laredo. He is the sheriff's brother. You are in big trouble I think," the bartender said looking up at Selman.

"He went for his gun. I didn't want to shoot him so I hit him over the head."

"Yes, and you hit him hard I think...he is dead."

"What; he couldn't be? I just hit him with my gun barrel," Selman said quickly.

"If I was you, Senor, I would not stay here too long. The sheriff is not going to be very pleased, I think."

"He pushed the fight; that ought to account for something."

"I don't think so. The sheriff is not one you want to mess around with."

"Great, it's not bad enough that I've got a sheriff on my trail for shooting his brother, now I've got another one; and then there's Sackett who thinks I shot *his* brother," Selman grumbled under his breath.

"The sheriff will be coming to have lunch with his brother, Senor; if I was you I would...," the bartender started to say and then stopped in mid sentence.

"Who is riding that horse out there with the T bar T brand on it," a man's voice called out from the barroom entrance. That question, however, was followed almost instantly with, "What's happened here, Manny?"

"Your brother tried to shoot this man, but the man hit him and he is...how you say, unconscious...I think."

"Unconscious, huh," the sheriff said as he walked over to where his brother lay, while eyeing Selman all the time.

"I didn't want to draw down on him, Sheriff, so I hit him with my gun. As he fell he hit his head on the bar," Selman explained.

The sheriff bent over his brother's still body and felt for a pulse. After several seconds he looked up at Selman with a frown on his face.

"He's dead...you killed him."

"I didn't mean to, Sheriff; I was just trying to avoid a shootout with him."

"So you say," the sheriff said as he stood up and pulled his pistol from his holster. "Did any of you see what happened here," the sheriff asked the three other patrons in the bar?

They all shook their heads negatively which brought a deeper frown to the sheriff's face, "I should have known you would be deaf, dumb, and blind. Well, come on, hombre, I'll have to lock you up until I can find out exactly what happened here. You could be in a lot of trouble."

"I tell you I'm innocent of any wrong doing here, Sheriff," Selman stated firmly.

"Oh, and I guess you just found that horse you're riding out there, huh? That horse was reported stolen by the owner of the T bar T not one week ago. Now I'd say things don't look real good for you, hoss. Hand over your gun."

Selman handed over his gun and the sheriff marched him down the street to jail, but not before sending for the local undertaker to remove his brother's body. Once he had locked Selman up he closed and locked the front door of the sheriff's office and hung out a sign "Out to Lunch."

Walking over to the gun rack mounted on the wall, he picked up a two foot long riot club that was sitting next to the rack. He slowly walked back to the door that separated the jail cells from the outer office and opened it.

He stopped in the doorway and stared at Selman for several seconds, pounding the club into his open palm as he glared at his prisoner. Selman looked at the sheriff questioningly. Once he understood what was about to happen he backed into a corner of the cell and shook his head no.

"You're not going to use that thing on me, Sheriff. I didn't go looking for trouble; your brother did. I'm not about to stand here and let you use that club on me," Selman said through clenched teeth.

"I'm gonna beat hell out of you, boy," the sheriff said quietly as he moved towards the jail cell, still slapping his open hand with the club.

16

Brian Sackett reined his horse up to the hitching rail in front of the Laredo Sheriff's Office and stepped down. He wasn't at all impressed with the town of Laredo, but was glad to be here since he had a strong feeling this is where he would catch up with Selman. He was right, but not in the way he imagined. Things were fixing to explode like a cannon blast.

BJ pushed the door open and walked into the office. The sheriff was sitting at his desk, rocked back in his chair, balanced on the chair's back legs, and eating a plum. He looked at Sackett for a moment and then his eyes widened. He couldn't believe what he was seeing. Brent Sackett had just walked into his office as big as life; or so he thought; buy why? The sheriff didn't move.

"Howdy Sheriff, I'm looking for a man by the name of Myron Selman; have you heard of him by any chance?"

The sheriff slowly let his chair settle back so that all four legs were resting on the floor as he eyed the man for whom he had just tacked a wanted poster on the wall.

"Why are you looking for him," the sheriff asked cautiously?

"I want to take him back to Abilene to stand trial for shooting my brother. I've been on his trail for weeks now. I followed him to San Antone, but he gave me the slip," BJ said never taking his eyes off the sheriff.

"What is your name," the sheriff asked?

Brian cocked his head to one side slightly, "BJ Sackett...why do you ask?"

"Oh, just curious...you said you're looking for uh, who was it again," the sheriff asked, not having allowed Selman's name to register, because of who he thought had entered his office?

"Selman, Myron Selman," BJ repeated.

The sheriff shifted forward in his chair as he recognized the name as that of the man whom he'd arrested for killing his brother. He'd found his name on a note that he'd found tucked down in Selman's pant's pocket.

"Yeah, I just might know of Myron Selman. At least I arrested a man whose first name was Myron. He's dead," the sheriff related.

"Dead... Are you sure the man's name was Myron Selman?"

"Like I said, he had a note that started out, 'Dear Myron' and it was signed by a woman...uh...Gina, that's what it said."

"How did he die, Sheriff?"

"He beat my brother to death in a barroom brawl; he hit him with his gun and killed him. I arrested him and he tried to escape and I hit him with a riot club and killed him...accidentally of course," the sheriff said as he slowly rose to his feet.

"Well, I'll be hanged? If that don't beat all; here I track him all the way down here and find out that he's dead. Well, I guess I can go back home with a clear conscience," BJ said with a frown.

"I guess so, uh, Brent...isn't it," the sheriff asked?

BJ gave a questioning look at the sheriff. Again, someone thought he was his twin brother. Could it be that Brent was known here in Laredo also?

"No, Brent was my twin brother; I'm Brian Sackett, but I go by BJ most of the time. Do you know my brother?"

"You mean to tell me you have a twin brother?"

"That's what I just said. He was killed in the War. At least we think he was killed. But, maybe he wasn't. Have you seen a man that goes by the name of Brent Sackett?"

"No, I never actually met him, but if you will step over here I'll show you a picture of him. You can tell me if he is your identical twin brother or not," the sheriff said and pointed towards the wanted posters.

BJ walked over to the wall and stared at the top poster. It had Brent's photo on it all right. BJ's eyes widened at the knowledge that his brother was alive; at least it appeared that way. With the reception he'd received in Crystal City he felt sure that his brother was indeed alive.

Turning his back on the sheriff to view the wanted posters gave the sheriff the opportunity he was looking for. He whipped out his gun and cocked it; the clicking sound caused BJ to turn quickly around.

"Don't go for your gun or you're a dead man," the sheriff snapped.

"What's this for," BJ asked?

"Twin brother; killed in the War; what kind of a fool do you take me for anyway, Sackett? It looks like your bravado got you caught, boy. Now drop your guns, nice and easy," the sheriff said.

"I told you I'm Brian Sackett. Do you think I'd really walk into a sheriff's office if I was the man on that poster? I came here looking for the man you say you killed. If you'll send a telegram to the sheriff in Abilene he'll vouch for who I am."

"I know who you are, Brent Sackett, and I know that there's a reward on your head. Now drop the guns or I'll drop you," the sheriff said with a wave of his pistol.

BJ slowly unbuckled his gun belt and let it drop to the floor. So much had happened since he walked into this sheriff's office that his head was swimming. He had to get his thoughts together and quick.

The sheriff walked about three paces behind BJ as they moved towards the door that led to the jail cells. BJ knew that this sheriff was bent on getting the reward that was being offered for the capture of Brent. He doubted that the sheriff would even send a telegram to Abilene, but he was going to keep pushing the issue.

"Look, Sheriff, I'm telling you that you've got the wrong man. The sheriff in Abilene can straighten this whole thing out with one telegram. You've got to give me that much...a telegram," BJ pushed.

"Get over there," the sheriff said when they reached the cell he would house his prisoner in.

BJ stepped back away from the cell door making the sheriff move up to open it. The sheriff only then realized the door was locked. In his haste to unlock the door he accidentally dropped the key. For just a split second the sheriff's eyes went to the fallen key ring which was all that BJ needed.

With a mighty swift, hard kick, BJ kicked the hand the sheriff was holding his pistol in, sending it flying across the room. When it hit it the floor it discharged since the hammer was cocked back. The report seemed extra loud inside the confined area.

BJ threw a hard right hand that landed flush on the sheriff's jaw. A hard knee to the groin area and the sheriff doubled over. BJ hit him a hard punch to the back of the head and sent the lawman face first to the floor. The sheriff was out cold.

BJ quickly unlocked the cell door and dragged the sheriff into the cell. He closed and locked the door then hurried to the outer office and grabbed his gun belt off the floor where he'd dropped it. He headed for the door, but stopped about halfway there. Looking around quickly at the wanted posters he hustled back to the wall and grabbed the one bearing Brent's photograph.

So as not to arouse suspicions, BJ mounted up and rode out of town at a leisurely pace towards the border. He knew now that he'd have to head into Mexico for awhile. He quickly laid out a route for returning to Abilene that would be the safest for him to travel. He would cross over into Mexico, head up to Ciudad Acuna and then cross over to Del Rio. From there he would head on up to San Angelo and from there to Abilene. Once he was home he could straighten out all this mistaken identity mess.

BJ hoped the sheriff remained unconscious until he'd crossed the border in Nuevo Laredo. Hopefully no one would enter his office. There was a border guard stationed on the road that passed into Nuevo Laredo, but he was too involved with a Mexican senorita to be interested in one lone American cowboy.

Once safely across the border on the Mexico side BJ kicked his horse into a full gallop and headed along the Rio Grande in a north/westerly direction. He was low on supplies, but couldn't take the chance of stopping and buying any. He hoped he might find a small trading post along the way.

Brent reined his horse to a halt at the top of a small hill and took a long look back. Once he was convinced there was no dust trail being kicked up by the gang of bandits, he turned his attention more towards the north. After a couple of seconds he looked at his traveling companions.

"This is where I leave you boys, I reckon," Brent said without any change in his expression.

"What do you mean...you're parting company with us," Nagle asked with a frown?

"Yep; I've changed my mind about going to Monterrey. I think I'll head north to Amarillo. I just remembered a little gal that lives there that I'd like to see one more time before I check out," Brent said thoughtfully.

"Well, it was your idea to go to Monterrey. I ain't got a hankering to go there anymore than to... well...Amarillo. What say we tag along with you?"

Brent grinned at Nagle's reasoning. He liked Nagle, but wasn't all that crazy about Winkler. He saw the younger man as a half wit that might go off like a stick of dynamite if handled wrong. As far as having them tag along with him, he liked the idea. He knew the Mexican bandits were still back there, he could feel it. He still liked the idea of having three guns instead of merely his.

Brent picked up the pace as the three headed north in the direction of the Rio Grande. He hoped to lose the men who were trailing them, but didn't want to wind their horses in the process. He figured on doing a little reconnaissance to see just how close the gang was getting to them, but that would come as night began to fall.

They rode the rest of the day and found a small creek where they could make camp. While Nagle and Winkler set up the campsite, Brent rode back in the direction from which they'd come.

Brent kept to the hills rather than take the easier, more level route. He knew the gang, if they were still following them, would be sticking to the flat land. He had traveled about two miles when he first spotted the gang.

Because the sun was setting the gang had made camp for the night. Brent figured he'd wait until night had fully fallen and then do something that would slow them down. If he could spook their horses, it would go a long way in ending the pursuit. He found a spot where he could leave his horse, and waited.

As soon as the sun had gone down behind the western range of mountains, Brent made his way on foot down the hillside and up to the gang's encampment. He crawled along on his stomach keeping a watchful eye for the guards he knew the leader would have posted. He spotted the first one guarding the horses. He saw another one perched on a rock that would offer him a good view of the camp.

Brent moved slowly and quietly along the ground edging ever closer to the man guarding the horses. He was just about to make his first move when something caught his attention. Off to his right he saw a tumbleweed move. There was no wind, however, so what caused it to move? He waited.

After a few seconds he saw another tumbleweed move forward towards the campsite. Slowly he turned his head so he could look to his left. Two more tumbleweeds moved a good six feet towards the camp.

More movement from other tumbleweeds; the campsite was surrounded by Indians who were using the tumbleweeds as cover. Brent continued to lay motionless. In a few seconds all hell was going to break loose and when it did he would back track as fast as he could to where he'd left his horse.

He didn't know what tribe of Indians these were, but figured them to be Comanche. The Comanche made war against all travelers passing through the land; be it white, Mexican, or other Indian tribes.

The glow from the campfire cast a yellowish/orange hue over the area. Because of the size of the fire it made it near impossible for those inside the glow to see the movement that was taking place in the deep shadows around the camp.

Suddenly a loud scream that sent cold chills down Sackett's spine filled the night air. The Comanche warriors sprang into the camp from all sides, yelling and killing as they attacked. Shots rang out as the bandits tried to defend themselves, but they were simply over whelmed and over powered.

Brent didn't waste any time. He quickly jumped to his feet and ran away from the campsite bending very low in the process. When he got to a point where he could see his horse still tied where he'd left it, he straightened up and sprinted towards his mount. When Brent was about twenty feet from his horse, another blood curdling yell sounded.

A Comanche warrior leaped from a rock where he was hiding, and landed on Sackett. The two of them fell to the ground, locked in combat. Brent had a firm grip on the Comanche's right wrist; the hand that held the tomahawk the Indian was trying to use on him.

The two men rolled on the ground, each trying to get the upper hand. First one would be on top and then the other. They continued rolling around until Brent got atop the Indian and braced himself. This gave him much better leverage and allowed him to wrest the tomahawk away from the warrior.

With a mighty swing Brent hit the Indian in the head with the tomahawk. He felt the Indian go limp under him, but continued to hit the man several more times. Once satisfied the man was dead, he got to his feet. Just as he did another scream from behind him caused him to turn just in time to see another brave running towards him.

The Indian had made his presence known several yards too soon, because Sackett was able to draw his pistol and shoot the charging warrior. The Comanche brave fell about six feet from where Sackett was standing.

Not wasting any time, Brent raced to his horse and quickly untied the reins. He swung into the saddle and kicked the horse into a full run. As he rode away he could still hear the screams coming from the camp. He looked back but saw no one giving chase to him; he'd escaped unharmed.

It appeared they wouldn't have to worry about the bandit gang any more. Now, however, they would have to be on the alert for Comanche. Once Brent reached their campsite, he told the others about the attack and they doused the small campfire they had started. They would have to take turns standing guard through the night.

Meanwhile, back at the bandit gang's campsite, the killing was over and the entire gang had been wiped out; with the exception of one man, that is; Jorge Santos. He had managed to sneak away when the attack first started. He hid in the underbrush while the rest of his gang was being slaughtered. All he could do now, though, was wait until the Indians finished with the victory celebration and the pillaging of the meager belongings of the gang members.

The Comanche celebrated for over an hour, firing the guns they had taken off the dead men into the air and drinking what little Tequila they found in a couple of the dead men's saddlebags.

Santos saw a horse that had belonged to one of his gang members, no more than a hundred yards from where he lay. He knew, however, it would be foolish to try to make an escape at that particular time. He'd have to be patient and hope the horse wouldn't wander off too far. He kept a close eye on the animal.

Around midnight the Indians began to fall asleep. As far as Santos could tell they didn't even post a guard. He knew it was time to make his move. Slowly he moved from his place of hiding and towards the horse that was still no more than one hundred and fifty yards away. He bent low as he moved; picking his way very carefully. This was no time to get careless or make a mad dash for the horse.

As Santos neared the animal it raised its head and looked at him. He held one hand out towards it, hopefully to steady it and keep it from moving away. The horse bobbed its head up and down a couple of times, but didn't try to bolt

Santos took hold of the bridle and quietly climbed aboard. He gently urged the horse on while bending low out over its neck. The horse walked silently away from the campsite and the sleeping Comanche. Once he figured he was out of earshot, Santos kicked the horse into a full gallop and headed back in the direction of Laredo. He would remember the Gringo, however, who had killed his cousin. One day their paths would cross again, and when it did he would take his revenge. But now he would have to go about putting together another gang.

17

BJ Sackett rode along a hilltop near the Rio Grande until he saw where it formed a small pool at the bottom of the hill. He rode down the hillside to the river where he watered his horse and then tied the reins to a shrub at the water's edge. Looking around he figured to be totally alone so a refreshing dip in the pool would be a welcomed comfort.

He slipped off his shirt and pants and, wearing just his long johns, waded out into the water. It was cool; partly because the morning sun hadn't had a chance to heat it up yet. BJ enjoyed soaking in the pool, while noticing the soreness of his muscles slowly ebbing away.

He had been in the water no more than five minutes when he heard voices coming from beyond some tule reeds. It sounded like women's voices. He swam slowly back in the direction where he'd left his clothes and gun.

Before he reached the spot where he'd left his belongings he heard a loud splash of water as if someone had plunged into the pool. Within a few seconds he saw the person who had made the splash. It was a woman; then he saw another woman; two beautiful women; one with blond and one with pitch black hair.

The two ladies didn't see BJ at first, but when they did their eyes widened in surprise. After a brief moment the blond haired woman spoke.

"Oh, we didn't know someone else was using the pond," she said almost apologetically.

"There's plenty of room for the three of us," BJ said with a grin.

The two women looked at each other and chuckled.

Then the one with black hair replied, "I can see that, but what about five of us?"

Just then there were more splashes made. A second later two more women joined the first two.

"Who are you talking to, anyway?" a cute little auburn haired woman asked?

"Him," the blond said, pointing in BJ's direction.

A woman with light brown hair then swam into view. She smiled widely as she eyed the young man at the other side of the pool.

"Well, well, look what we have here," she said in a delighted voice with a strong Southern accent.

"Where are you ladies headed, anyway," BJ asked, actually wanting to know.

"Why, we've been combing these hills for weeks just looking for you, Honey Child," the Southern belle said, drawing a laugh from the others.

"Well, I'm glad you found me," BJ responded.

"Actually we're on our way back to San Antonio. We have been down to Monterrey...uh, entertaining some gentlemen," the one with auburn hair stated.

"Oh, I see. Well, lucky for me that I just happened to be here at this time, huh," BJ said with a laugh.

"It could be, cowboy," the blond replied.

"You're not traveling alone, I hope," BJ asked thoughtfully?

"Oh, no; in fact we've got a couple of guardians traveling with us," the black haired woman said.

"Yeah, us," a man's voice said off to BJ's right.

BJ looked and saw two men standing next to his clothes...and gun. He could tell these men were hired guns simply by the way they wore their hardware. A sudden uneasiness came over BJ.

"You boys are a little far west of the trail to San Antone aren't you," BJ asked?

"I don't think so. We heard there was some trouble with Comanche down south of Laredo. We sure don't want to run into a band of Comanche."

"Who does," BJ replied?

"Where are you headed, stranger," the taller of the two men asked.

"I'm on my way up to Abilene...Texas," BJ answered.

"I think you should come out of the water and let the ladies enjoy their baths, cowboy," the shorter man said in a surly voice.

"I was just about to do that," BJ said giving the man a hard, steady gaze.

BJ looked towards the women who were watching what was taking place with the men. He looked back at where his clothes were and then back at the ladies.

"You ladies want to turn your heads while I get out of the water," Sackett said in a pleasant voice.

The women looked at one another and then back at him.

"No," the blond said with a smile.

"I beg your pardon," BJ replied.

"I said 'no' we don't want to look the other way while you get out of the water," the blond repeated.

"Okay; have it your way," BJ said and started for the bank.

He began walking out of the water when a shot rang out and hit the shorter of the two men in the chest. The man fell backwards and before he hit the ground another shot rang out. The bullet from the second shot kicked up a puff of dust next to the taller of the two men who dived for cover.

The women screamed and began swimming towards the tule reeds. BJ quickly moved into the reeds to be somewhat hidden from the sniper fire. He made his way around so he could get to his clothes, but mostly wanted to reach his gun. Two more shots rang out, but didn't hit anyone.

"Can you see where the shots are coming from," BJ called to the tall man?

"Yeah, from some rocks up on that hillside," the man replied.

"Can you tell how many are up there," BJ questioned.

"I think there're two, maybe three, but I can't be sure. They're out of range of our handguns though, I know that."

"Do you have a long gun with you?"

"Yeah, a couple, but they're in the wagon."

BJ found a branch that was long enough to reach his clothes. He pulled them over to him and got dressed. The branch wasn't strong enough to lift his gun belt so he would have to risk moving into the open in order to get it.

Making a quick lunge for the gun belt drew two more shots from the ambushers, but both shots missed. BJ's horse was too much in the open for him to try and get to his Winchester, but he might be able to get to the wagon the man had spoken about.

"I'm going to make my way through these tule reeds to where your wagon is. I'll bring you a rifle back," BJ said to the man.

"Go for it," the man replied.

BJ worked his way through the tall tule reeds to where he could see the wagon...and the ladies. They were hunkered down behind a large rock; naked as jaybirds. When they saw BJ they tried desperately to cover their nakedness.

"Do you mind looking the other way," the little blond said.

"No..," BJ replied with a grin.

"What," the blond replied?

"I said 'no' I won't look the other way," BJ said showing a little 'gallows humor.'

Looking from the women to the wagon he saw that he could be halfway to it before he would be out in the open. He made a mad dash for the wagon and was almost to it before a shot was fired. The bullet barely missed.

Once he was behind the wagon he was able to pull the canvas covering up and climb inside. He found four Winchesters and six boxes of shells. He grabbed up two rifles and two boxes of shells and climbed back out through the side.

He made another quick dash towards the tule reeds and was able to get there drawing only a single shot from the ones on the hill. Making his way back behind the reeds he reached the spot where the tall man was still pinned down.

"Here," BJ yelled and tossed the man a rifle followed by a box of shells.

The two men now had guns that would reach the men on the hillside; if they could only get a glimpse of them, that is. BJ eyed the hillside carefully. Suddenly he saw a man appear at the top of the hill attempting to run over the crest. Another man started on the same course as the first man had, but had more ground to cover.

BJ took careful aim and slowly squeezed the trigger. The rifle bucked in his hands and the man on the hill side stiffened, standing straight up. He turned around facing the pool, and fell face forward down to the ground. The bullet had hit him squarely between the shoulder blades.

"You got him, pardner," the tall man called out.

Before BJ could answer another man emerged from the rocks on the hillside and ran towards the downed gunman. He was yelling something as he ran, but when he reached the downed man, stopped. After a few seconds the man got up again and began walking towards the pool yelling and firing his rifle as he walked.

The tall man raised his rifle and fired one shot. The man on the hillside stopped in mid stride. BJ started to fire, but didn't. The man on the hill put his hand to his stomach and then removed it. Slowly he sat back in a sitting position dropping his rifle to the ground as he did so.

"You got him," BJ said as he heard the man jack another shell in the barrel. "Don't shoot him again; let's take him alive if we can. I'd like to know why they ambushed us."

"The women more than likely; these bandits down here love the ladies."

"I don't think these two are Mexican bandits. They look more like Gringos to me."

The two of them slowly moved out into the open, but with their rifles ready just in case the other two bushwhackers were still up there. Cautiously BJ and the other man moved around the pool and up the slope. As they drew near to the wounded man he opened his eyes and looked at them. He had been gut shot and was dying.

"Why'd you try to ambush us," BJ asked?

"Horses...money...women," the man struggled to say.

"Who are you, anyway?"

The man took a painful deep breath and swallowed hard, "The name's...Nagle; Charlie Nagle."

Just then he raised his eyes and looked into BJ's face.

"You...you," Nagle said when he saw that BJ looked exactly like the man he knew as Dan Johnson.

"What is it," BJ asked?

Nagle coughed, spitting up some blood as he grew more and more weak.

"You look...exactly like....Johnson...Dan Johnson," Nagle said haltingly.

"Dan Johnson; and you know this man Johnson," BJ asked?

"He was the one...who led...this ambush against you," Nagle said and then began coughing again.

"Where were you headed," BJ urged?

"Amarillo that's where we..." Nagle started to say, but never finished. He slumped to one side and died.

The tall man looked at BJ and shook his head, "I wonder what he meant by that? It was obvious he thought you were someone else for a moment...this Dan Johnson fella."

"I've been told before that I look like someone else," BJ said as the question once again filled his mind; was Brent still alive and now going by the name of Dan Johnson, or not?

18

Brent kicked his horse into a full gallop as he left the hilltop and headed on towards the spot where he would cross the border into the U. S. He wanted to put as much space as he could between himself and the ones he, Nagle, and Winkler had tried to ambush.

He would have to find a fresh horse somewhere else. His was beginning to limp a little when the terrain got rocky. He couldn't afford to be stuck out here in this godforsaken country afoot.

He didn't have to wait long before he got another chance. He spotted a small herd of cattle headed north by six cowboys, probably on their way to the railhead. They would undoubtedly have a small ramuda from which to exchange their mounts; a ramuda that would supply him with the fresh horse he needed.

Brent rode up to the man riding point. The man eyed the stranger approaching the herd warily at first, but when he was convinced the man was alone visibly relaxed.

"Howdy, what's up," the point man asked?

"I'm on my way up to Abilene; to the railhead. That wouldn't be where you're headed would it," Brent questioned, figuring that was where the herd might be headed.

"Nope, we're headed to the railhead in San Antonio," the man replied.

"You mean they have a train there now," Brent asked feigning ignorance?

"They have for some time. Where've you been, anyway?"

"Deep in the heart of Mexico," Brent lied.

"Oh, taking on those senoritas, huh," the man grinned.

"Yeah, love their enchiladas," Brent said with a laugh.

"Oh, is that what they're calling it now," the man replied.

Brent laughed and then changed the subject.

"Say, you wouldn't need another hand driving these cattle would you?"

"I thought you were headed to Abilene?"

"Not if there's a railroad in San Antonio, I'm not," Brent replied.

The man pointed back towards the middle of the herd, "You'll have to talk to the trail boss; he's the one riding the sorrel back there. If you've moved cattle before he might take you on; we lost one man two days ago."

"Thanks...I've been in a few cattle drives," Brent said with a wave as he kicked his horse up and headed in the direction of the trail boss.

The trail boss was a stocky man of about forty years with a hard look due to the hard work he had done most of his life. Brent rode up to him and nodded.

"Howdy, I heard you might be in need of another drover; is that right?"

The trail boss gave Brent an appraising look before answering, "Yeah, that's right. Have you ever driven cattle before?"

"A few times; I know what I'm doing if that's what you're driving at."

"It is," the man said, and then added, "I can only pay you a dollar a day and another one for every day you've been with us when we get the cattle delivered."

"That's twice as much as I'm making right now," Brent said with a grin. "I'll start right away. Where do you want me...riding drag?"

"How'd you guess;" the man said as he grinned slightly, "I guess you have moved cattle before."

BJ looked at the four women and their lone protector and shook his head. He almost felt obligated to see them on to San Antonio safely, seeing as how the other guard was now dead.

"You wouldn't consider going on to San Antone with us, would you, pardner," the tall man asked.

"Yeah, okay; I'll tag along with you to San Antonio. I can alter my route that much I guess," BJ said.

"I do appreciate it," the tall man said. "By the way, my name is Cletus Cameron. And who might you be?"

"I'm BJ Sackett, from up Abilene way. Nice to make your acquaintance," BJ said as the two men shook hands.

He didn't really want to go to San Antonio, but maybe he should to inform Selman's fiancé of what had happened and to assure her that he had nothing to do with his death. He figured she would still blame him though, because Selman was running to get away from him.

The wagon containing the four women, with Cletus driving, moved slowly along the narrow, but well traveled road on its way to San Antonio. BJ rode alongside the wagon, but couldn't get his mind off the fact that several different people, people that didn't even know one another, had confused him with another man that they said looked exactly like him. If Brent was still alive, BJ would love to see him and tell him to come on home where he belonged.

At that same time, Brent was riding drag behind five hundred head of cattle on their way to market. He figured he would have to leave Texas eventually because of everything that had happened over the past month, and that would be hard to do, since he truly loved his Texas.

What would he do once they arrived in San Antonio; if he decided to go all the way with the drive, that is? For the first time Brent began to have a twinge of conscience about some of his past actions. He began to wonder how Ben Cates wife had taken the news of her husband's death. Then he remembered how she had shared her bed with him when Ben had to go to Fort Worth to bring back a prisoner to stand trial.

She had made plays for him before, but he had always deflected her advances. That one time, however, he had given in and she had held it over his head from then on. She could no longer threaten him with that bit of old news, not now; not with Ben being dead. Besides that was small potatoes compared to his other 'crimes'.

He thought about the other sheriff he killed in Encinal. Had the man been married? Did he have children? These and other thoughts begin to crowd his mind. He thought he'd hardened his conscience to a point of not really caring about other people's feelings or welfare. Maybe he'd been wrong. One thing he knew for certain though; he was a man on the outside of the law and on the run. Whatever he might regret now, it was too late to do anything about it.

So the two identical twin brothers both made their way towards San Antonio; one with a herd of cattle and the other with a wagon loaded with prostitutes. What would happen when the two arrived there? Would they meet each other? Would fate keep them apart after having brought them so close together? Only time would tell. And a lot could happen along the way.

One thing was certain, however, and it was something for which both men were thankful. They were across the Rio Grande now and once again on beloved Texas soil.

The End

Across the Rio Grande

Printed in Great Britain
by Amazon